More Praise for *Mariette in Ecstasy:*

"Hansen gives back to the world the complexity and beauty of its existence—those elements of life that make us call it a creation—in a language spare and mysterious enough to capture the ambiguities of devotion and the sensuality of faith."

—Mirabella

"The sleeper hit of 1991...Hansen writes to inspire awe. And by veiling the inside, he suggests that there may be mysteries greater still, probably even more luscious and strange than what you can see with your bare eyes. Whatever one might think of this as religious instruction, as fiction it is terribly seductive."

—Village Voice

"Explores the most profound questions of spirituality...with writing so lovely it seems to ring. Open the book anywhere, at random, and the writing takes your breath away."

—Orlando Sentinel

"Engrossing. Hansen writes a beautiful prose."

—Newsweek

"None of [Hansen's] mysteries are neatly resolved—and the biggest one may be the degree to which one finds oneself passionately yearning for the miraculous."

—The New Yorker

"The shortest novel I have read this year is also the best....If Mariette is in ecstasy, so is Hansen's prose, a miracle in itself.... We are spellbound."

—The Nation

Mariette in
Ecstasy

ALSO BY RON HANSEN

Desperadoes

*The Assassination of Jesse James
by the Coward Robert Ford*

Nebraska

For children

The Shadowmaker

Mariette in Ecstasy

Ron Hansen

HarperPerennial
A Division of HarperCollins*Publishers*
An Edward Burlingame Book

The Library of Congress has catalogued the hardcover edition as follows:

Hansen, Ronald, 1947–
    Mariette in ecstasy / Ronald Hansen.—1st ed.
        p.   cm.
ISBN 0-06-018214-8 (cloth)
    I. Title.
PS3558.A5133M37   1991   813'.54—dc20   90-56362

ISBN 0-06-098118-0 (pbk.)
92 93 94 95 96 AC/CW 10 9 8 7 6 5 4 3 2 1

to my mother, Marvyl

Directoire des religieuses
du Couvent de Notre-Dame des Afflictions

Le nom	La responsabilité	L'âge
Reverend Mother Céline	Prioress	37
Mother Saint-Raphaël	Mistress of Novices	65
Sister Catherine	Extern Sacristan	81
Sister Saint-Pierre	Gardener	74
Sister Ange	Equerry	66
Sister Agnès	Extern Laundress	62
Sister Anne	Extern Sexton	60
Sister Saint-Denis	Religion Teacher	59
Sister Monique	Cellarer	57
Sister Marthe	Cook	55
Sister Emmanuelle	Seamstress	54
Sister Honoré	Choirmistress	50
Sister Marguerite	Librarian	48
Sister Saint-Estèphe	Candlemaker	46
Sister Saint-Léon	Cook	46
Sister Antoinette	Winemaker	45
Sister Marie-Madeleine	Carpenter	40
Sister Saint-Luc	Extern Farmer	40
Sister Dominique	Cook	37
Sister Virginie	Winemaker	36
Sister Saint-Stanislas	Milkmaid	34
Sister Véronique	Arts Teacher	33
Sister Sabine	Extern Milkmaid	30
Sister Zélie	Extern Farmer	30
Sister Félicité	Winemaker	29
Sister Aimée	Infirmarian	27
Sister Saint-Michel	Farmer	27
Sister Philomène	Novice	25

THE WINTER LIFE OF THE
SISTERS OF THE CRUCIFIXION

2:00	We rise in silence, go to choir, recite Matins.
2:30	Meditation, followed by Lauds.
3:00	Sleep, reading, or private prayer.
5:00	Second rising.
5:30	Prime, followed by Low Mass.
6:30	Mixt.
7:00	Work. The Great Silence ends.
9:00	Terce. High Mass on holy days.
9:30	Work or classes.
11:30	Sext.
12:00	Angelus, and dinner in silence.
1:00	Méridienne. Exercise or rest.
2:00	Nones.
2:30	Work or classes, or recreation on holy days.
4:30	Reading or private prayer.
5:00	Vespers.
5:30	Meditation.
6:00	Collation.
6:30	Recreation.
7:00	Chapter and Compline.
8:00	We all go to bed. The Great Silence begins.

Part 1

Upstate New York.

August 1906.

Half-moon and a wrack of gray clouds.

Church windows and thirty nuns singing the Night Office in Gregorian chant. Matins. Lauds. And then silence.

Wind, and a nighthawk teetering on it and yawing away into woods.

Wallowing beetles in green pond water.

Toads.

Cattails sway and unsway.

Grape leaves rattle and settle again.

Workhorses sleeping in horse manes of pasture.

Wooden reaper. Walking plow. Hayrick.

*   *   *

Limestone pebbles on the paths in the garth. Jasmine. Lilac. Narcissus.

Mother Céline gracefully walking, head down.

Crickets.

Mooncreep and spire.

Ears are flattened to the head of a stone panther waterspout.

OUR LADY OF SORROWS
ERECTED 1856
CHURCH AND PRIORY OF
THE SISTERS OF THE CRUCIFIXION

Tallow candles in red glass jars shudder on a high altar.

White hallway and dark mahogany joists. Wide plank floors walked soft and smooth as soap.

Sister Dominique says a prayer to Saint Peregrine for her Canadian nephew's cancer as she dashes flour on a kitchen table and turns over a great slab of dough that rolls as slowly as a white pig.

Sister Emmanuelle hunches over a pink sewing cushion, her quick hands tying off bobbins and pins as she creates lace periwinkles for the white corporal that the holy chalice will rest on.

*   *   *

4.

On the prioress's great pecan desk, a red Latin missal is shut upon a five-dollar bill. Tasks are written on a paper held down with a jar of India ink and a green fountain pen. Envelopes from patrons have been neatly slit open and are shuffled up in a blond wicker basket.

Sister Sabine is in a jean apron as she strolls toward the milking barn between Guernsey cows, her hands riding their caramel hides. She smells her palms and smiles.

Wings batter and bluster. Tree branches nod and subside.

East and the night sky gradually deteriorating. A nickel light is just above the horizon.

Sister Hermance waits in the hallway outside the sisters' cells. In her right hand are wooden castanets. She peers at a silver chatelaine watch that is attached to a waist-deep neck-lace of black satin ribbon. She pauses until the hour is precisely five. She then hoists her hand high, clicks the castanets twice, and cleaves the Great Silence by shouting, "In Jesus Christ, my sisters, let us rise!"

She hears six or seven sitting up and sleepily responding, "His holy name be praised!" and she walks down to the hall-way's turning.

Sister Aimée stays lying on her palliasse just one more moment. She then gets up and hates the morning before ach-ingly getting to her knees on the floor in order to pray an Ave Maria.

Mother Saint-Raphaël tugs her plain white nightgown up over her head. She is hugely overweight but her legs are slight as a goat's. Tightly sashed around her stomach just below the great green-veined bowls of her breasts are cuttings from the French garden's rosebushes, the dark thorns sticking into skin that is scarlet with infection. She gets into a gray habit, tying it with a sudden jerk. She winces and shuts her eyes.

Waterdrops from the night's dew haltingly creep down green reeds.

A rabbit skitters forward in the priest's garden and twitches a radish leaf with its nose before tearing it loose. Ears tilt as it hastily chews and settles over its paws.

Eighty years old and shrinking with age, his wrists as thin as pine kindling, Reverend Henri Marriott is sleeping in his house just outside the sisters' cloister, twisted up in his nightshirt, a hissing kerosene lamp still lit, a book of philosophy skewed beneath his left arm. His soft white hair is harrowed and wild and his week-old white beard is stained faintly with food. Teetering against his neck is a gold cross botonnée that he got at his first Mass in Louvain, Belgium, fifty-five years ago. When the porter raps twice on the house door, the priest wakes up with a sudden inhalation, a "huh" of astonishment, and then he hears Sister Anne trespass inside the house and sidle up to his bedroom door and pause and ask him, "Are you truly up, Père Marriott?"

"Yes. Completely."

"You have High Mass today, too. You should shave."

She is just four years a widow. She wifes him out of habit. Henri Marriott says a prayer, as always, for Sister Anne's late husband, then sits up and tests his feet on the floor planks.

She asks, "Will you need our help getting dressed?"

With pain in his joints, he stands up and totters to his

dresser, putting his hands flat upon it before saying, "Your priest is much better today, Sister Anne."

"We are so pleased," she says, and goes away.

Sisters who are still in their nightgowns and gray flannel robes are bent over the great tin washing bowls, rinsing their mouths and spitting, or soaping their hands and faces. Just to their left are sisters standing next to the indoor privies with demurely lowered eyes. Here alone there is one mercury-plated looking glass, which is no larger than a windowpane and hanging in a plain wooden frame. Sister Pauline is peering at herself in it as she tucks her hair and pins on the soft white veil of a novice, and then she sees Sister Saint-Léon just behind her shoulder signing *Too long, here, you*. Sister Pauline shrugs her regret and Sister Saint-Léon jots a note on her hand pad.

Reverend Mother Céline stands patiently in the vestibule just beside a sixteenth-century painting of the Annunciation. While the sisters get into their positions for the solemn entrance into the oratory for the canonical hour of Prime, the prioress does not speak but smiles or raises her hand slightly in greeting, and then she goes to her place next to Mother Saint-Raphaël and the great brass bell in the campanile rings.

Wooden doors open and the sisters walk in pairs from the nave into the great hall of the oratory just to the south of the high altar. Each genuflects to Christ in the tabernacle and then turns away to go to her assigned seat in choir stalls that are tiered like jury boxes.

Sister Léocadie hurries down the hallway, holding up the skirt of her white habit. She slows in the nave and humbly enters.

*   *   *

Everyone is in her pew seat and contemplating the high altar behind the oakwood grille. Sister Léocadie goes immediately to Mother Saint-Raphaël, the former prioress and now mistress of novices, kneeling just before her and kissing Mother's pew railing as she confesses her lateness and penitence. Mother Saint-Raphaël gives the novice an irritated nod but no penance, so Sister Léocadie prostrates herself facedown on the floor until her shame has passed.

The prioress stands up and says, "We shall pray now for our new postulant." She kneels and so do thirty-one nuns. Everyone is upright on the kneeler, getting no support from the pew, her hands in prayer just below her chin. When there is pain each will offer it up for the wretched souls in purgatory whose sins have kept them farthest from God.

Henri Marriott recites vesting prayers in the priest's sacristy as he turns up the hem of the ironed white alb that Sister Catherine has laid out and socks his hands into great sleeves that are as needleworked as doilies. With pain he ducks his head inside the alb and wriggles it over himself like a nightshirt. His strict precise Latin ticks from his mouth as he rectifies the hem of his shoes and ties the white rope cincture at his waist. Mademoiselle Baptiste, he thinks, and then scowls at Sister Catherine's uncertain writing on the intentions card for the Solemnity and tries to remember the girl's Christian name. Mariette Baptiste.

She is upstairs in a great country house and sitting at a Duchess desk in a pink satin nightgown as she pens instructions to the housemaid, saying to whom her jewelry and porcelains and laces and gowns ought to go.

She then stands and unties the strings at her neck so that

the pink satin seeps onto a green Chinese carpet that is as plush as grass. And she is held inside an upright floor mirror, pretty and naked and seventeen. She skeins her chocolate-brown hair. She pouts her mouth. She esteems her full breasts as she has seen men esteem them. She haunts her milk-white skin with her hands.

Even this I give You.

Dr. Claude Baptiste stands at a kitchen window in red silk pajamas, drinking chickory in the sunrise, looking outside as if his hate were there, hearing Mariette just above him.

GOD THE MOST HIGH

Supreme Being and Creator

of Heaven and Earth and

OUR LADY THE BLESSED VIRGIN MARY

Mediatrix and Queen

of the Court of Heaven

Kindly Request Your Presence at the Spiritual

Wedding of Their Son

JESUS

Our Lord and Redeemer

to

MARIETTE BAPTISTE

When She Asks to Be Received

into the Sisters of the Crucifixion

on Wednesday, August 15th, 1906,

the Feast of Our Lady's Assumption into Heaven.

Mixt. Café au lait and a hunk of black bread that Sister Ange soaks in her great coffee bowl before she toothlessly chews. Sister Saint-Denis squashes her left forefinger down on the white tablecloth and sucks the dark crumbs from it.

And then work.

White sunlight and a wide green hayfield that languidly undulates under the wind. Eight sisters in gray habits surge through high timothy grass that suddenly folds against the ringing blades of their scythes. Mother Céline stoops and shocks the hay with twine and sun-pinked hands.

Four novices stand taciturnly at a great scullery table plucking tan feathers from twenty wild quail shot by a Catholic men's club just yesterday. Horseflies are alighting and tasting the skins, or tracing signatures in the hot air.

Sister Marguerite is in the scriptorium at a twelve-person library table, squinting at a text and then scratching a pen across a coarse sheet of paper as she translates into English *The Constitution of the Second Order of the Sisters of the Crucifixion in Accordance with the Common Observance of the Rule of Saint Benedict.* She tries a sentence to herself and writes, "When there is nothing else which we ought to be doing, it is our sweet obligation to pray."

Extern Sister Anne is still huffing breathlessly in the campanile as she grins up at the pigeons shuffling along the rafters and frantically jerking their heads toward her. She gets a handful of sweet-corn kernels from her gray habit's pocket and scatters them on the flooring, and the pigeons heavily flap down and trundle around her sandals. She then reads the time on her late husband's railway watch and grabs the chime pulls with hard brutal hands, heartily summoning her sisters to the hour of Terce and High Mass.

White cottages and a shaggy dog tucking its nose in four parts of a juniper hedge and then trotting on. Chimes for High Mass are ringing at a great distance and a girl is eating toast on a milking stool outside the general store. She glances up the road, sucking jam from her thumb, and gets to her knees on the green porch.

Mariette Baptiste is in solemn procession to the Church of Our Lady of Sorrows in her mother's wedding trousseau of white Holland cloth and watered silk. Trailing the postulant on horseback or phaetons and carriages are girlfriends and high school classmates and villagers.

Dr. Baptiste is not present.

She has hoped for an hour's peace and contemplation on the way to the church, but she is blessed or praised or spoken to by a hundred people and she is given pink and white nasturtiums wrapped in a flute of parlor wallpaper. She thanks the people by smiling or touching their wrists or fleetingly laying her hand on a baby's head.

—Were you happy to have so much attention?

—Well, no. I had been hoping to present myself to the sisters with Christ's own plainness and humility.

—But you got instead a pageant.

—Yes.

—And you thought your sisters were passing harsh judgment?

—Even then.

While she and her grand company enter the public side of the church and she walks up the white runner to the prie-dieu, she thinks the sisters are passing harsh judgment and that she must seem too spoiled and rich and vain to take their holy vows; but she kneels and peeks behind the great oak grille to her right and sees that the sisters praying there in the oratory have given no sign of dislike or disillusionment and only the slightest hints of having even acknowledged her presence.

Mass of the Solemnity of the Assumption
of the Blessed Virgin Mary.

Mother Saint-Raphaël is sitting in choir just above her five novices, her frowning pink face all puckers and creases, and she stands with the others when their freshly shaved priest haltingly walks from his sacristy for the holy sacrifice of the Mass. At the introit she stares at the too-pretty postulant and is surprised to see that she's weeping with happiness. And she is pleased, too, that this Mariette gives such active and rapt attention to the readings and preface and consecration, kneeling heedfully upright, perceiving each meaning and connotation, tenderly following the holy chalice as it is raised up and presented. *She's twenty pages of a book; she's half an hour of teaching.*

Sister Honoré gestures a pause and then floats her right hand again as she guides the sisters through the *"Pange Lingua,"* tilting a little to hear the girl who's asked to join them. She gets another hint of the new postulant's song, hearing a fair soprano who tightens her throat on the higher notes and slightly mispronounces the Latin *c*, but seems more practiced than half the novices. She briefly glances at Mariette as she turns another page of the score, and then thinks unwillingly of Sister Alexine, a girl from Strasbourg to whom she taught English, who was expelled from the Motherhouse just before solemn vows because she'd tattooed the Sacred Heart on her heart with purple ink and a hairpin. The choirmistress hushes the contraltos with her hand.

Sister Philomène is again besieged with such distracting thoughts and temptations and disloyalties that she prays before she knows she is praying and she kneels before she knows why. Whereas their new postulant seems such a picture of meekness and holiness and awe as she walks up to receive the Host, that Sister Philomène makes it her Communion prayer that God in His patience and kindness would one day choose to give her, His worst sinner, the grace to be just like Mariette Baptiste.

And then when the High Mass is done, the old priest turns and tentatively eases himself down to the railing again in order to say to the church, "Who asks to be received into the grace and blessings of the religious life as handmaid of the Lord?"

She feels their stares like heat. The postulant stands up from her white-flowered prie-dieu and says, "Mariette Baptiste."

"Will she now come forward?"

She kneels at the railing as Père Marriott heavily lays his hands on her head and prays to himself in a hoarse whisper before announcing to the public, "Here is Mariette Baptiste whom God has called to Himself. She is putting away the things of this world, giving up her earthly pleasures, perishing out of season. Say adieu to Mariette, whom you have called your niece, your cousin, your friend, your classmate, your confidant. Say adieu to the girl you knew but did not know, the girl you have loved but not as soon nor as much nor as well as her Creator has loved her; the soul that is turning now from Satan's pomps and empty promises and toward Christ's service and true promise of eternal life. She is the child born into a sinful world but on this great day she is dying into the holy life of the Sisters of the Crucifixion, and the intercessions of Our Lady of Sorrows, the care of the Christian saints and martyrs, the wisdom and comfort of the Holy Ghost, and the everlasting peace of Our Lord."

Everyone in the Church of Our Lady of Sorrows then walks up to Mariette and kisses her or tenderly pats her hands or asks for remembrance in her prayers. And she sees her father standing in misery by the first station, where Christ was condemned, his forearms crossed over his hot suit and vest, his eyes as red as noise. She goes to him in order to say goodbye, but Dr. Baptiste hurriedly walks away and ducks outside into heat. She turns to the high altar and hears the choir singing the "*Te Deum*" and sees the old priest inviting her forward with both hands, and she realizes that he has opened the green marble Communion railing. She passes through with joy, without glancing back, genuflecting to Christ in the tabernacle and going to the hidden door of the grille that Mother Céline is holding ajar.

"Welcome, Mariette," the prioress says, and kisses her on each cheek. And then the Sisters of the Crucifixion step down from their places in the choir and one by one greet Mariette with slight embraces and words of encouragement, until she's touched by a green-eyed troll of a woman who was a truck gardener in the village before she joined the order as an extern at the age of fifty-six.

Sister Agnès grins up at the new postulant as she whispers, "We'll be saying the Litany of Our Lady now, Mariette. You come get your things."

"It's Mar-iette."

"What did I say?"

"Mare-i-ette, like a horse. It's Mar-iette, like a flaw."

"Easy to remember, isn't it," Sister Agnès says.

She takes Mariette to the haustus room just next to the refectory and she smiles as she skates her hand over a white fluting of watered silk. "Such a pretty dress."

"Annie wore it when she asked to enter."

"Who?"

"Mother Céline. She's my sister."

Sister Agnès just smiles.

"Shall I take it off?"

"Yes; of course. And your shoes and stockings. Everything." Sister Agnès then goes out, saying she'll return in a Paternoster.

Mariette diffidently takes off her shoes and stockings by tilting onto one foot and then the other, for there is no parlor furniture in the haustus room, only a grand piano, gray stone walls, prettily stained windows, and a great painted Christ on a crucifix. She uneasily gets out of her dress and underthings and she is a girl again, four years old and staring at the Christ in her mother's room. She touched his pink mouth, the pink rent in his side, and then she touched her own mouth. She touched underneath her skirt.

She kneels on the oak plank floor.

—Was she in ecstasy, Sister Agnès?

—You ask too much of a simple woman.

—Would you please describe what you saw?

Sister Agnès hunches along the hallway skidding a ship's trunk just ahead of her sandals, then knocks softly on the haustus room's door and tows the ship's trunk inside.

Mariette is kneeling on the floor, unclothed and seemingly unconscious as she yields up one hand and then the other just as if she were being nailed like Christ to a tree.

*   *   *

Mariette hears the door gently touching shut and sees Sister Agnès sidling toward her with green eyes shyly on the floor and a great bulk of black clothing held against the wide gate of her hips. "Excuse me," she says, "but I have duties. Eight hours a day you pray."

With some embarrassment, Mariette stands up from the floor and hides her nakedness from the extern as Sister Agnès wordlessly takes the new postulant's dress and crinolines from her and Mariette gets into a black muslin habit that smells richly of potash soap, then steps into some black rope sandals and knots a black rope cincture at her waist. She says without certainty, "Done," and only then does Sister Agnès peer at her.

"Everything fits?"

She pauses. "You wear no underthings or stockings?"

"We dress simply here in summer. Your feet are too cold?"

She shakes her head.

"Your first winter is the hardest. Chilblains and pneumonia. Even with the furnace on. Externs have it easier there. We live in the old calefactory."

"Where's that?"

"Just outside the true priory, next to the visitation parlor. We're widows, us externs, or we have pasts, or we don't have educations, so we please God by praying a little less and serving Him a good deal harder." She peers sideways at the new postulant as she seems to revise what she was prepared to say. "Mariette Baptiste. Your family have French in them? You can speak it?"

"Some."

"And you can read, too?"

She nods.

"Ho, you'll be one of the pets then. Especially for the old ones and them that's just here from Brittany. My job in the convent is, I think you say, *blanchisseuse.* Which is?"

"Laundress."

She smiles with odd mirth and hands Mariette a torn and too-often folded sheet of paper dated 1901 and headed, *"Trousseau personnel d'une soeur de la crucifixion."* Written in underneath is an inventory of twenty-one items that Mariette translates for the extern as Sister Agnès hunts in the trunk for another *habit noir,* the hardwood work shoes called *sabots,* one cotton and one flannel *chemise de nuit,* and handkerchiefs, old wool stockings, hand-knitted gloves, a great black cape, and a gray bathrobe with a tattered hem and a faint bloodstain on the front. And then Sister Agnès withdraws a black scarf from the trunk and gets on her tiptoes to float it over the girl's hair, speedily tying it behind Mariette's ears just as a kitchen witch would, just as Mariette has seen a fruit picker do after having intimacies with a foreman in tree shade.

Sister Agnès grins at her shame and says, "You are Christ's peasant now."

She then stands apart from the new postulant and says in a practiced way that their Reverend Mother insists that the sisters have purity and cleanliness uppermost in their daily thoughts. The convent should be spotless, the gardens tended, the air free of stink and smoke and noise. Each is to change her habit every few days and wash herself with soap at night just before Vespers and again upon rising so she will not be infested. She is not to adorn her hair. She is not to tempt the sin of pride with perfumes or rouge or time misspent at the mirror. Especially, she is not to tempt their holy priest with pretty wiles and movements and flattery as Satan may invite a young woman to do. She should expect loneliness and sadness and illness and hard use. She should expect, too, that she will be tempted to have particular affection for some of her sisters. Such affections are not permitted. For Jesus Christ ought to be their grandest passion, just as *la sainte volonté de Dieu,* God's holy will, ought to be their only desire.

"Have you understood Mother's holy rules, Mariette?"

"I have."

"You're quick, you are. Your eyes say so. Have you any questions?"

"When will I be cutting my hair?"

"You'll keep it as a postulant, just as you'll keep your own name. You do things right and one day in six months or so, you'll join us as a novice, and you'll get your religious name and we'll all have fun with the scissors. And now this poor old sinner will have to go prepare your feast, and you'll have to be going to the infirmarian to prove that you're a virgin."

She is taken to the infirmary by a sweet, fat, toad-eyed novice named Sister Hermance who trundles ahead of Mariette down a hallway, skimming her knuckles along the white walls, and then slows after a turning until she's walking next to the postulant. She hides her mouth behind her hand to confide, "Have you begged God to grant you a great thing today?"

Mariette just looks interestedly at her.

"When I joined the order I prayed to go away from home and have home totally forget me. I have been praying since for humiliations and hardships and perfect atonement for my sins. And perhaps, too, consumption and an early death." She thinks for a second or two and asks, "Is it *too* much, Mariette?"

She shrugs. "I have been praying to be a great saint."

Sister Hermance peers at her seriously. "Such pride, Mariette! You surprise me."

She smiles. "I'll try to be irresistible."

Sister Hermance goes ahead again. "We will be silent together now." And at another turning she invites Mariette to go past her into a six-windowed and snow-white infirmary equipped with two empty beds and another in which Sister

Saint-Pierre is asleep on her side, a headscarf flattening her frail cloud of white hair.

Sister Aimée is at a scoured porcelain sink, rinsing a tray of silver pipettes and scissors and tweezers with hot water from a teakettle. She fleetingly looks at the postulant, then puts the teakettle in the sink and unpins her gray sleeves over forearms and hands that are orange with freckles. She glimpses Sister Saint-Pierre as she whispers, "She has a stomach complaint. American wine, she says. Are you okay?"

"Yes."

"Have you been ill at all this past year?"

"No."

"Ever?"

"Just as we all are."

"Your mother died how?"

"Cancer."

Sister Aimée says, "*Requiescat in pace,*" and considers a two-page medical report that is atop a stack of white pillows and gray woolen blankets. "So you're Mother Céline's sister."

"She's twenty years older."

"Amazing." She frowns at an item and flatly says, "Headaches?"

"Occasionally."

"Trouble sleeping?"

"I shouldn't have mentioned it."

"Are you taking medications?"

"No."

She turns a page and looks up from the signature. "Dr. Claude Baptiste. Your father?"

"You have to go forty miles for another."

"Wasn't it awkward being examined by him?"

"Yes."

Sister Aimée stares at her, and then she says, "I just got here from Maryland. I haven't met him." She reads a sentence and turns to the postulant again. "Will you please show me your nails?"

Mariette holds out her hands and Sister Aimée dents the pink of a nail until it whitens. "You have to get permission to fast from our prioress or from Père Marriott in confession. And of course that is also true for trials and mortifications. Will it be possible for you to work at hard labor?"

"I hope so."

"Me too," Sister Aimée says, and she pens a note on a blank line. "Are there foods you don't eat?"

"No."

"Are there extremes when you menstruate?"

She shrugs.

The old woman weakly asks for help in French and Sister Aimée hastens to her.

Mariette shies her eyes away as Sister Saint-Pierre is rolled to her back, and she peruses a tall blue-paned cabinet of tiered pills and balsams and ointments. Each has been classified under an adjective: Alexipharmic, Anesthetic, Antipyretic, Cathartic, Emetic, Epispastic, Soporific. Everything else is placed just where it would be in her father's surgery. She hears Sister Aimée say in French that the new postulant is here, and Mariette turns to see Sister Saint-Pierre sitting up a little and smiling at her with gray teeth. A half-century gardening in hard sun and weather has spiderwebbed her skin with wrinkles.

"*Enchantée, Soeur Saint-Pierre,*" Mariette says. "*Comment allez-vous?*"

"*Malade, mademoiselle. L'estomac.*"

"*Je vous plains.*" I'm sorry for you.

Sister Saint-Pierre shrugs and says, "*Tout pour Jesus.*" Everything for Jesus.

Sister Aimée goes back to her medical forms and jots a note, then regards Mariette with great seriousness as she asks, "Will you please take down your hair?"

Mariette unties Sister Agnès's knot in the scarf, untwists and unplaits the tight chignon at her nape, and shakes her chocolate-brown hair loose.

Sister Aimée walks up to Mariette and says, "Excuse my familiarity," and fully inspects the new postulant's hair and skin and teeth. And then she stares out at green spruce trees as she presses her thumbs and fingertips along the girl's jaw and throat and gently probes both breasts. She says, "We have heat and hot barley tea here in the winter if you get too cold. We also have some herbs and powders and syrups. And that's all. The idea of having me as a doctor adds to disease a new terror." She pauses. "We pray you stay healthy."

"And you, Sister."

"Thanks." While Mariette puts her black headscarf on again, Sister Aimée takes up the medical report and tosses it on a desktop. She says, "And now I think Sister Hermance will show you to your cell."

Mariette hesitates until she sees that Sister Saint-Pierre is again sleeping. She whispers, "Weren't you going to ask if I'm a virgin?"

Sister Aimée assesses Mariette. "I assume you are?"

Mariette says nothing and then she says, "Yes."

"Isn't that interesting," says Sister Aimée, and she simpers as she puts towels away.

Sister Hermance grins as she greets her again. "I have been trying not to hear," she says. She's holding a rosary as she hurries down the hallway.

—She is in love with you. Our Sister Hermance.

—Is it true? Well, yes. I see now. She has a very great heart.

*　　　*　　　*

Mariette's cell is a nine-by-nine room just down the hallway from the oratory, with one eastern window with a bleared and pebbled and watery view of green pasture and flourishing woods that hold a slow river in them as a hand holds a stick. Whitewash has been painted over the plaster walls but the joists and high ceiling planks are shellacked oak and mahogany. A fractured and hoof-scarred tack room door has been nailed to two sawhorses and a palliasse of straw placed on top for the new postulant's bed, just as in the other rooms. White cotton sheets and a child's feather pillow are tucked underneath a taut blanket made of gray felt. White paint hides the hundred-year-old wood of a tilting pine armoire that stands as high as she does. Next to Mariette's palliasse on the floorboards are a tin basin holding a tan block of soap and an ironed towel, and an hourglass, a box of tallow candles, and a great porcelain water jug that is as blue as a patch of noontide sky, she thinks, and the only pretty color in the room. A holy water stoup is next to the doorjamb, and just a few feet above Mariette's pillow is a hideous Spanish cross and a painted Christ that is all red meat and agony.

She has been given a Holy Bible, a red prayerbook she can slip into her pocket, and an English translation of *The Way of Perfection*, Saint Teresa of Avila's handbook for contemplative prayer. She has not been given a pen or ink or paper or so much as a scrap of mirror. She has been given nothing to sit on. Even on this hot summer day she cannot get used to the coldness of the floor.

Sister Hermance scuttles about the cell giving titles to the furnishings and illustrating how they're used, as if Mariette's head is filled with feathers. She seems to be playing house in a bossing way as she teaches Mariette how she ought to hang her few things inside the armoire, arranges Mariette's hairbrush and toothbrush and nail file and scissors, and jams a brick into a door that—against the rules—insists on shutting.

She solely talks to make certain that Mariette under-
stands that she is only to *sleep* on the palliasse; she is not to
sit or pray or weep on it, she is to touch it no sooner than
eight at night and get up from it at once when the sisters rise
again at two for Matins and Lauds. She tells Mariette that
the sisters observe a Great Silence from Compline at night
until just after Mixt. She says Mariette ought to try to think
of sleep as an illness that the sisters are cured of with the
Night Office and again at dawn. She ought, too, to try to
empty her head of possessions and the pronouns *me* and
mine. "Everything in this room is *ours*. Even you, you are
ours now."

"And Christ's."

She smiles at Mariette hesitantly just as the Angelus bell
slowly rings. Sister Hermance turns in the general direction of
the high altar and gets to her knees as she prays, "The angel
of the Lord declared unto Mary."

"And she conceived of the Holy Ghost."

And then an Ave Maria is said.

Sister Virginie is kneeling with scissors and hyacinths in
the garth but she tenderly puts them on the grass as she says
to herself, "Behold the handmaid of the Lord."

Sister Marie-Madeleine holds on to a ripsaw and brushes
wood shavings and dust from her gray habit as she privately
gives the response, "Be it done unto me according to Thy
word."

In the kitchen the sisters stand by the hot stoves in
rolled-up sleeves, their white aprons stained with soups and
juices, steam from saucepans wetting their chins. Sister Saint-
Léon's hands are whitely gloved in flour as she prays for the
rest, "And the Word was made flesh."

Cook's helpers with her respond, "And dwelt amongst us."

The prioress stands at her desk, her palms held up to her face as though she's in tears. She says, "Pray for us, O Holy Mother of God." And then she replies in antiphon, "That we may be made worthy of the promises of Christ."

Sister Hermance smiles as Mariette recites from girlhood memory, "Pour forth, we beseech Thee, O Lord, Thy grace into our hearts, that we to whom the incarnation of Christ, Thy son, was made known by the message of an angel, may by His passion and cross be brought to the glory of His resurrection. Through Christ Our Lord. Amen."

Sister Hermance holds on to the pine armoire as she wrestles up onto her sandals and steps into the hallway. Seeing that Mariette is not following, she turns and touches her five joined fingertips to her mouth in the handsign for eating.

Wild quail in spiced vinegar are served along with hot bread and green peas and a *grand cru* wine from the Haut Medoc. And Sister Saint-Michel is in a great tree of a pulpit high above the dining room, just beginning the weeks-long *Lectio Divina* of Dame Julian of Norwich's *Revelations of Divine Love*. She announces, "Chapter Two. The time of the revelations, and Julian's three petitions."

"Dame Julian writes: 'These revelations were shown to a simple and uneducated creature on the eighth of May 1373. Some time earlier she had asked three gifts from God: one, to understand his passion; two, to suffer physically while still a young woman of thirty; and, finally, to have as God's gift three wounds.' "

Six refectory tables are arranged so that the sisters sit nearly against three walls that are as white as an unwritten page. Effaced and still and interior, the sisters do not talk and do not turn from their food and do not raise their eyes from their dishes as kitchen workers in white aprons hush their way from place to place, setting down saucers of red grapes and browning pears and soft goat cheeses.

Mariette is sitting at the main table between Mother Céline and the mistress of novices, Mother Saint-Raphaël, and she peeks at their hands now and then to ensure she's doing the things she's always done in the religious and grammatical way.

Sister Saint-Michel reads: " 'The second petition came to me with much greater urgency. I quite sincerely wanted to be ill to the point of dying, so that I might receive the last rites of Holy Church, in the belief—shared by my friends—that I was in fact dying. There was no earthly comfort I wanted to live for. In this illness I wanted to undergo all those spiritual and physical sufferings I should have were I really dying, and to know, moreover, the terror and assaults of the demons.' "

Half the priory is staring up at the reader with fascination and horror when the prioress says, "*Satis.*" Enough. And Mariette sees Sister Saint-Michel obediently shut the book as the older sisters immediately put down their forks and iron out their napkins with their palms. They all stand up for Mother Céline's prayer of thanksgiving and then walk out in silent pairs.

Méridienne. Sister Catherine and Sister Saint-Estèphe are in Empire chairs in the chapter room. A briarwood ship's clock ticks on the fireplace. Window drapes of Chantilly lace flush and deform on the breeze. Sister Saint-Estèphe's black veil pleats against a chartreuse head pillow as she sleeps. Sister Catherine's hands are turned up on her knees. Each withered palm is a pink nest of wrinkles.

*   *   *

Eight professed sisters amble through horsetail grass as high as their thighs. Hundreds of yellow butterflies are scheming through the field and alighting on their gray habits. One sister points to a woodpecker and another shades her eyes but cannot find it. Talk. One sister pokes her teeth with a grass stem. And then the wildest sister rejoices and whirls and flumps down in the horsetail. Even at a distance their rich laughter peals like piano notes.

Crows hunt the shade of green corn and pant in the hot sun with open beaks, as if holding prized huckleberries.

A marmalade tomcat is sitting in his haunt by a nesting place in the old sheep's meadow. Yards away the still woods drowse with insect whine and the chirr of cicadas, and his tail rises and idly settles, his green-yellow eyes become slits.

Mariette is sitting in hot tree shade, chasing gnats with one hand while she pursues another rosary bead and prays for humility. Elegant Sister Saint-Léon is lying back on her elbows in short bluegrass nearby, trying to teach the new postulant a history of the religious order that she already knows. Sister Saint-Léon dries her forehead with a handkerchief she keeps on her wrist with a rubber band and she tells Mariette in French that the Comtesse de Rossignol used her great wealth to organize the Sisters of the Crucifixion nearly two hundred years ago in Dijon. Their Motherhouse is now in Louvain. Even today they are not a large order; hardly three hundred nuns are listed in their *directoire des religieuses*. She thinks the Sisters of the Crucifixion have been in Belgium and America since the properties of the religious orders were stolen just after that horrible revolution and in the Empire years. And then there were the harsh restrictions of the Waldeck-Rousseau laws in 1901. Thirteen of the sisters here have fled

France and arrived in this country since then. And what a purgatory it is for them.

Sister Saint-Luc walks up with a wreath of braided yellow dandelions that she crowns Mariette with as she kneels. Mariette bashfully smiles and asks her, *"Comme il faut?"*

"Très jolie," says Sister Saint-Luc. She is a simple and perpetually happy woman with skin as brown as cinnamon and blond hair on her upper lip and chin.

"We have been talking about the history, Luke."

Sister Saint-Luc says seriously, "I have the secret of how to stay in our order, Marie. Have you any idea what it is?"

Mariette says no.

"You must never ever *leave*," she says, and smiles so enormously that Mariette can see she has no chewing teeth.

Sister Saint-Léon sighs. "Saint Luke and I are cousins. We have nothing else in common."

"I have been her disciple since I was three," says Sister Saint-Luc. "She has been my penance." And then she gives the postulant a handwritten note from the prioress. "She says you are expected."

While the others have another half hour of recreation, Mariette is sent to the prioress's suite, next to the visitation parlors and the house of the extern sisters. She waits for Mother Céline on a flowered ottoman and takes affectionate stock of a grand office that has plush heavy chairs, a pink velvet sofa with four chintz pillows, two brass floor lamps with tasseled lampshades, and old newspapers from Paris and New York City and Rome draped over bamboo sticks. Everything removed from the scriptorium is here in a high wall of science and economics textbooks, French and English romances and poetry, old treatises on histrionics and phrenology and animal magnetism.

She hears horses pass the convent at a trot. She hears

under that four or five stringed instruments being practiced down the hallway. Schubert, she thinks. She gets up and opens *The Ethics of Belief* and abstractly turns pages until Mother Céline hurries in like a regal woman of property, going over what are apparently a kitchen inventory and some sisters' notes that she's just been passed. Without irritation she says, "I have entered the room."

Mariette smiles uncertainly.

"Curtsy."

Mariette does.

"We say '*Benedicite Dominus*' in greeting. The Lord bless you. You'll say '*Benedicite*,' and the superior nun will say, '*Dominus*.' Upon leaving one's company or classroom, you'll hear the superior nun pronounce, '*Adjutorium nostrum in nomine Domini*.' Our help is in the name of the Lord. And you'll reply, '*Qui fecit coelum et terram*.' Who made heaven and earth."

"Yes, Reverend Mother."

"Sit down, please," the prioress says, and Mariette complies.

Mother Céline seems a glamorous actress playing a nun, or one of the grand ladies of inheritance that Mariette has seen in paintings of English society. Without her black veil and gray habit, the prioress would seem a genteel and handsome mother of less than forty, blond and lithe and Continental, but tense and initiating, too, with green eyes that seem to strike what they see. She was Annette Baptiste and a junior at Vassar when Mariette was born, Sister Céline and a novice when their mother died, the prioress of Our Lady of Sorrows since Mariette was twelve. She arranges and grooms her papers on the green felt of the desktop and then she briskly sits opposite Mariette and puts her hands on her knees as she asks, "Are you happy?"

"Oh yes."

She smiles. "We're happy, too. Every new postulant affirms our own vocations and gives efficacy to our prayers."

"Everyone has been very nice."

"We must seem to talk and feast all the time."

Mariette shakes her head. "I presumed today was an exception."

"We aren't meant to pine away and die here. We're meant to live in the heartening fullness of God. Who is life and love and happiness."

"I know."

"We seem to mystify people who are slaves to their pleasures. We often work too hard and rest too little, our food is plain, our days are without variety, we have no possessions nor much privacy, we live uncomfortably with our vows of chastity and obedience; but God *is* present here and that makes this our heaven on earth. We hope you'll find the same welcome and peace here that we have, and that you'll soon develop a genuine and reverent affection for our priory and for your sisters. We pray, too, that soon it will seem you've given up very little and, as always with our good God, gained a hundredfold."

Everything seems practiced, as if she has said just this to a half-dozen other postulants, but Mariette pleasantly listens and says, "Oh, already I feel that! This is paradise!"

Mother Céline smiles but stares discerningly at her sister for half a minute. And she asks, "Are you and Father still on good terms?"

"Yes."

"Is there a reason why he wasn't present for the ceremonies?"

Mariette pauses before saying, "Papa is a good man, I think, but he has been against my religious vocation since I first began talking about it. He said he'd given the sisters his first daughter and he thought that was enough."

The prioress seems to be trying for sympathy, but her stare is tenacious and penetrates like a nail. "That must have been disappointing for you."

Mariette shrugs. "God isn't finished with him yet."

Mother Céline sits back in the assessing way of a jurist. She says, "I have a letter from Father that accuses you of being too high-strung for our convent. And he is troubled by gossip from friends and patients about trances, hallucinations, unnatural piety, great extremes of temperament, and, as he put it, 'inner wrenchings.' I have laid all that aside, of course, or you wouldn't be here, but I would like to hear what you have to say about his qualms and hesitations."

Mariette suddenly seems slow and dull and oddly abstract, like a wrong sum at the tail end of a child's arithmetic. She says, "I have forgiven him for them."

"Was he dishonest in his description?"

"I have no opinion, Reverend Mother."

"Was he duped then?"

She just stares.

"We won't be, Mariette. Secrets are impossible here. Your mistress, Mother Saint-Raphaël, will be watching you closely these next few months. You'll be put to test many times. We have wonderful plans and expectations for you, but you will have to prove worthy of them. Don't try to be exceptional; simply be a good nun. Saint Ignatius Loyola gives us the right prescription: Work as if everything depended on you, but pray as if everything depended on God."

"I shall."

"I'll take you to the oratory now."

—Were you surprised by the tone?

—She did seem cold.

—Were you hurt?

—Oh no! I was so pleased to see our dear God using my

sister for my own holiness and good. Everything seemed to be saying to me, *She will be a grace for you.*

Mother Céline rises up and holds open the door for the postulant before preceding her down the hallway. She grazes the stone with her knuckles as she says, "We try to walk these halls as silently as the Holy Ghost. And we stay close to the walls here in humility and in graciousness to our sisters who may be talking with God."

Sisters Honoré, Saint-Denis, Véronique, and Philomène are gaily leaving the haustus room with their violins and viola and bows tucked underneath their arms. Sister Saint-Denis sees the prioress and gravely curtsies, and then the choirmistress and the others do, too.

Mother Céline half raises her hand in blessing and asks, "What was that you were practicing?"

"Franz Schubert," Sister Honoré says. " 'Death and the Maiden.' Was it good, Reverend Mother?"

"Oh indeed. Wonderful. You resurrected her."

Wild, high-strung, deferential laughter follows, and Mother Céline frowningly turns from it.

Troughs of sunlight angle into the oratory like green and blue and pink bolts of cloth grandly flung down from the high, painted windows. Still present are the wood oil smells and habit starch and an incense of styrax and cascarilla bark. Mother Céline and her postulant genuflect together and Mariette's right knee touches down on a great red Persian carpet that seems as warm as a sleeping cat. She sees faint gyres of dust in the hot upper air.

The prioress says, "We praise God in song here seven times a day. At two a.m. for Matins and Lauds, and then for the first, third, sixth, and ninth hours of the day: Prime, Terce, Sext, and Nones. We then have Vespers at sunset, and Compline after collation and just before bed. Every week we go through the whole Psalter. Sister Honoré plans to teach you the rudiments of plainchant next week.''

Mother Céline walks forward to the right-hand choir while she tells her sister, "Externs, novices, and postulants are the first to enter. You all kneel in the first rows." She puts her hand on the second stall in from the upper end. "You'll be here, Mariette."

Mariette exultantly walks around to her stall, sitting testingly in it and skidding both hands along its shined rail. She kneels and prays for greater religious fervor and that the joy she feels now will comfort her in the difficult times ahead. And then she feels the prioress kneel beside her and finds only kindness in Annie's eyes.

She asks Mariette, "Were you called just recently?"

"Early," she says. "Continually. Ever since my confirmation God has been persuading me."

Mother Céline fondly touches a hand onto hers and holds it there. "We must thank Our Lord for the honor of inviting both of us to serve Him here."

"I shall. Every day."

"Seeing you here is such a pleasure for me."

Mariette smiles. "I have missed you so much."

Mother Céline withdraws her hand from her sister's. "I'll seem subdued and distant. We'll hardly ever talk. You'll think I don't love you because I won't show it." The prioress turns her head and then stands up. "Try to remember that I have many sisters in my family now. Don't expect too much from me."

At two p.m. the sisters join them in choir for Nones, but Sister Honoré tells Mariette not to join in the psalms until she has been taught the Latin and the ugly chains of square black notes that sing like the hymns of the seraphim.

She listens hard, however, just as she did as a child in the church pew, sitting with Dr. Baptiste on a holy day, smelling his iodine and tweed and Turkish cigarette tobacco, peering beyond the oaken grille at Annie or Sister Catherine or Mother Saint-Raphaël and hearing these same gray sisters in the yearnings and elations of plainsong.

When there's meditation and a shutting of the Psalters, Mariette looks up at the high west windows. Evangelists are represented in the ox with wings of Luke and the lion with wings of Mark, the high-soaring eagle of John, and Christ's genealogy in the human figure of Matthew. Opposite them in the upper east windows are Abraham, Moses, David, and Isaiah; and high above Our Lady's green marble altar to the south and its beautifully carved limewood Pietà from Germany is the glorious rose window and its iridescent peacock in violet, navy blue, and emerald green, a symbol of Christ's resurrection. She smells linseed oil and hard soap and frankincense and tallow. She is in a great room of thirty-three women, but she has never heard such silence. West from Mariette in the upper choir stalls Sister Ange, who handles the horses and whose mind has become a jumble, is grinning across the oratory and agreeably nodding encouragement, as if their postulant is a child newly toddling forward with a firm hold on her mother's forefinger. Sister Véronique holds tight to prayer, her full lips forming unspoken words, her half-glasses glinting silver. Sister Marie-Madeleine hunkers over her knees and hides her face in her hands while Sister Catherine hunches over a book just inches from her nose and harriedly hunts another page.

And Mariette thinks, *Here you are, and here you'll stay.*

Mariette is still saying prayers of thanksgiving in the oratory when Sister Geneviève kneels heavily next to her and after a Memorare says, "We have a secret place."

And Mariette is taken up to the campanile, where the hot wind has the pressure of hands. Sister Pauline is skulking up there already and getting on her tiptoes as she tilts out over the railing and says in an itsy voice, "We're being bad."

White sheep are in a green pasture, hardly moving, and at a great distance some Sunday farmers in dark galluses and white shirts and ties are slowly walking a blond hayfield and using red handkerchiefs on their high-button shoes. Everything slants up into hillsides of green fir and cedar and the gray-blue haze that slurs the horizon. A peregrine falcon is suspended on the air, hunting some hidden prey, and suddenly twists into a dive of such speed that Mariette loses track of it until the falcon has flared high up into the sky again.

Sister Geneviève is still huffing breathlessly as she shoos pigeons that are discussing their presence and waddling along the rafters. She is a great soft chair of a woman, frank and hearty and jolly, with sun-browned skin that is goose-bumped with pimples, and with gruesome nails that she tears with her teeth. She gives Mariette a sideways glance and asks, "Were you talking with Mother Céline earlier?"

She's puzzled but says yes.

Sister Pauline turns. "Oh, truly? You're so lucky!"

Sister Geneviève says, "She's beautiful, isn't she."

"She is."

"She knows we're up here. She knows everything. So does Mother Saint-Raphaël. Even what you're thinking."

"Especially about boys," says Sister Pauline.

"We talk about old boyfriends up here," says Sister Geneviève. "We talk about what we miss. Whiskers. Dancing. Everything."

Sister Pauline turns again to the railing. "We saw a whole picnic from up here once. We couldn't tell the girl's age, but the guy was a soldier. Wearing a tan uniform and those high boots and eating chicken with her on a green plaid blanket. And then kissing. She was nearly underneath him."

Mariette smiles tauntingly and says, "You don't suppose it was me, do you?"

Sister Geneviève grins. "You don't mean it."

"Was he handsome?"

"She seemed to think so."

"And tall?"

Sister Geneviève squints inquiringly at Sister Pauline. Sister Pauline seems to presume height, and then she's positive. Yes.

"Are you sure it was a *green* picnic blanket?"

"She's teasing us," Sister Geneviève says. "You're just trying to be mysterious, aren't you, Mariette."

She shifts her face from theirs and doesn't say.

"Oh, tell!" Sister Pauline cries.

"She's a kidder, Sister P. She's getting our goat."

And then Sisters Philomène, Hermance, and Léocadie join them and titter and talk as Mariette smilingly watches. She sees that everything is a subject, but never for long; great hurts are manufactured from slights; giggling is the general music; gossip is encouraged and told and then halfheartedly regretted. Sister Léocadie is a tagalong and an afterthought who seems to be forgetting a sentence even as she gives it her full attention. Sister Philomène is no sound at all, a tall and gentle intellectual with a skewed right eye who trembles fraily up there, like a flame. Sister Hermance seems plainly in awe of the others and wears the constantly surprised and stricken look of a girl who's just been slapped. "Mother Saint-Raphaël was pretty when she was a girl," she says. "You can tell by the way she carries herself."

Sister Geneviève says, "You can tell she was rich, is all. She carries herself like *she* was carried."

"Who?" Sister Léocadie asks.

Sister Pauline turns to Mariette. "Just try to stay on her good side."

"She'll love Mariette," Sister Hermance insists.

"Who are we talking about?" Sister Léocadie asks.

Sister Geneviève tells Mariette, "Mother Saint-Raphaël will take you aside someday and teach you about yourself and you'll turn out to be just like she was."

"She's been everybody twice," Sister Pauline says.

"She has great empathy," Sister Philomène says.

"She wasn't me," Sister Léocadie says.

Sister Geneviève looks at Léocadie for a hard second and the willowy novice withdraws inside herself.

Sister Philomène smiles abashedly at Mariette and says, "You'll love it here. Truly."

"You get stale though," Sister Geneviève says. "You get tired of the routine. We see the same people hour after hour. And you can predict just what they'll do."

"Even the finicky way they eat," says Sister Pauline.

Sister Geneviève continues, "We all begin to talk alike after a while. We have our periods at the same time. You look at some of the older nuns and you can hardly tell them apart. You're the gossip of the summer. Exciting things just don't happen here that often."

"Except in prayer," Sister Hermance says, and then hears a haughty piety in her tone and pinks in embarrassment.

Mariette looks out from the high window of the campanile to the horse paddock. Externs are there, simply talking. Sister Sabine lies back in blossoms and holds a hand up to block the sun. Sister Zélie is sitting with her knee up to her chin as she tends to a hurt toe. Sister Claudine is kneeling in wild oats and weeds that are tilting and striving under the wind. Here and there Mariette sees nuns on their own, sketching the old printery in the woods, gently toweling the glossy brawn of a chestnut-brown horse's neck, fishing the dull green pond with a kitchen string and a float, Sister Antoinette worriedly strolling the vineyard and holding the grapes like a half-pound of pearls. Sister Anne is sitting in the garth with Sister Virginie. She opens a railwayman's watch and gets up to hurry toward the campanile, but Sister Virginie shades her eyes and questions the sexton and she pauses. "Sister Anne's on her way," Mariette says.

"We're having a recital," Sister Philomène says.

"Shall we go then?"

Sister Pauline hesitates but says at last, "We wanted to touch your hair."

Mariette blushes and demurs until Sister Geneviève defends their asking by saying, "We've just cut ours." And so Mariette unties her scarf and shakes loose her chocolate-brown hair and she smiles with them as they tentatively float their hands over it and trail it out fluently on the wind.

Evening. She sets out the tin plates and tin cups for collation, then stands in the kitchen with a hunk of rye bread and soup bowl of cassoulet, and tilts close to the slightly ajar kitchen door in order to hear Sister Saint-Michel read Dame Julian of Norwich.

She hears: " 'When I was halfway through my thirty-first year God sent me an illness which prostrated me for three days and nights. On the fourth night I received the last rites of Holy Church as it was thought I could not survive till day. Since I was still young I thought it a great pity to die—' "

And then Sister Saint-Stanislas interrupts by touching the postulant's wrist and irritably making the handsigns, *Serve, priest.*

While Sister Dominique uses wooden paddles to shovel hot bread loaves from the oven, Mariette places a china plate on a teakwood tray and overlays it with green cabbage and an arrangement of tinned sardines. She goes to the great caldron and scoops cassoulet into a soup bowl that she centers on the china plate, then wraps a hot loaf of bread inside a white napkin that she ties into rabbit ears. She sticks a hand inside the indoor well and snags up a yard of twine. Twisting from the wet knot at the end is a trickling bottle of a blond Sauterne.

Sister Saint-Stanislas is standing over the tray, adding a china jar of wildflowers and the holy day silverware. She says in handsigns, *Eyes, no, priest.*

The priest's house is empty when Mariette taps on the ajar door and peeks inside, so she takes up books and papers from his dining table and sets out the dinner plates and the Sauterne.

She is pleased then to think of herself as the priest of the house and she walks about it handling the priest's soiled and cracked and floor-tossed possessions. She turns a kitchen lamp up. She feels the tin cold of an icebox and hears ice water trickling into the pan underneath. She tries a key on his black Blickensderfer typewriter and jumps a little at the noise. She strokes an orange mandolin with green detailing and pigtailed strings, and Dutch clay pipes and tamping nails and a jar of tawny tobacco. His books are French, Greek, and Latin philosophy texts; *A Child's Garden of Verses;* exemplary sermons by Pope Gregory XVI; French commentaries on Holy Scripture; books by Augustine, Duns Scotus, and Peter Canisius; fourteen volumes of Thomas Aquinas, but some with uncut pages; green-mildewed novels by Anatole France; *The Prisoner of Zenda;* a French translation of an Englishman's journey to Sicily and Malta; *Histoire de l'admirable Don Quichotte de la Manche.* She kneels on his prie-dieu and touches open his breviary. She recites aloud the first words of the fifty-first psalm, *"Miserere mei Deus."* Have mercy on me, O Lord.

And then she hears Père Marriott ask from the doorway, "*Latine legere scires?*" You know how to read Latin?

She blushes and puts the book as it was. "*Vix quicquam,*" she says. Little or nothing. She turns and sees the priest with his white collar unsnapped like a horseshoe, a tan suede of dust on his black riding boots.

Marriott stoops over the china plate and smells the tinned sardines. "But you know the idioms," he says. "You are being too modest, I think."

—And that is when you told me?

—Yes.

—Just for the record, how did you put it exactly?

"I have had an experience."

The priest raises up the Sauterne and holds it under a tasseled lampshade to read the appellation. "Yes; it has been a great day for you."

"Earlier," she says, and she pauses until her tentative silence causes the old priest to look up. She says, "Jesus spoke to me." She turns away from him and tries to halt her trembling with a hard embrace. She sees a wasp pulsing at a saucer on the floor and denting a white pearl of cream as it drinks. She says, "Ever since I was thirteen, I have been praying to understand his passion. Everything about it. To have a horrible illness so I could feel the horrors and terrors of death just as Christ did. And to have, too, his true contrition for our sins and his great love for us, his children. And yet each time I prayed to share in his hurt and torment, I have been put off by an interior voice saying my time had not come yet. And then one night I prayed to him about joining the Sisters of the Crucifixion. And oh it was wonderful!" She pauses. "Even now I can't talk about it. Whenever I have tried to in confession, I haven't been able to utter a word."

Henri Marriott smiles insincerely and scratches his hair as he stares at the jar of wildflowers and thinks. She is surprised by his pensive calm. At last he asks, "Was your priest sympathetic?"

She shakes her head no.

"Well then, I shall try to be." Edging around a dining table chair, Marriott gets tiredly onto it and sits with his heels on a rung. "Hear me, Mariette. You are not the first young nun to tell me such things. Especially now in the infancy of your religious vocation, Satan will be tempting you in a hundred ways. When you see Christ or hear Him, you must be mistrusting and wary, for Christ is a Word that does not give voice to the ear but goes directly into the mind. Jesus does not usually speak; Jesus performs and inspires. Also, He does not make Himself present to our human senses but in the holy desires of the will. Jesus impresses His form upon the soul and fills the heart with joy."

Mariette says nothing.

"Was it like that for you?"

She is mute.

"You must be wary, Mariette. You must stay out of Satan's eye and try to be pure and sinless. *Comprenez vous?*" You understand?

"*Oui. Je vous comprends. Merci.*"

—And you were given pen and ink.

—That's right.

—Would you please repeat why?

Marriott smiles as he walks to her from a book-jammed secretary, holding green fountain pen and ink bottle atop some sheaves of fine writing paper. "Each night, or when you have a little time, please talk to me in a journal or letters just as you would in confession. I have found such writing quite helpful for other postulants. And then simply deposit the letters in the prioress's mail slot. Try to remember to put on your envelopes 'Confessional Matter' or Mother Céline will perforce read them."

—So you were not instructed to lie or pretend?

—Exactly the opposite.

—You were not to make up stories? Or try to be interesting?

—No.

—Everything written to me should have been as solemnly true as the sins that you confess in the sacrament of penance.

—Everything was.

She gets into a plain white nightgown after Compline and kneels girlishly on the floor beside a trembling yellow candle flame. She crouches over a blank page with the priest's green fountain pen tentatively held above the paper as she thinks. She twists a chocolate-brown spill of hair over her head and stays it there with one hand as she touches the pen's nib down and then speedily writes, the pen slashing across the page without hesitation or correction.

Every day and in the midst of every kind of disobedience and failing, I have asked Jesus to have pity on me and either take my life entirely or, in his justice and mercy, give me a great deal to suffer in atonement for my own foolishness and the sins of the world. While there have been times when he permitted me to enjoy the greatest consolations, there have been times of darkness and silence, too, when I felt disliked and in disfavor and, with hopelessness and pining and tears, I prayed to Jesus from a place that was very near Hell.

You are my dearest and only father on earth now, Père Marriott, but we do not know each other so well yet that I dare say all that I have seen and heard and understood. Oh how I yearn to give you a place in my heart and confide in you and paint in their radiance all of my secrets and experiences! I have been forbidden, however, to do so. At this time I am only permitted to tell you that Our Lord has promised that I will suffer great pain in the course of my life. Christ has told me that soon he will put my faith to the proof and find out whether I truly love him and whether the offering of my heart which I so often have made to him is authentic.

Christ said, "You will grow hard, Mariette. You will find yourself afflicted and empty and tempted, and all your body's senses will then revolt and become like wolves. Each of the world's tawdry pleasures will invade your sleep. Your memories will be sad and persistent. Everything that is contrary to God will be in your sight and thinking, and all that is of and from God you'll no longer feel. I shall not offer comfort at such times, but I shall not cease to understand you. I shall allow Satan to harshly attack your soul, and he will plant a great hatred of prayer in your heart, and a hundred evil thoughts in your mind, and terror of him will never leave you.

"You will have no solace or pity, not even from your superiors. You will be tortured by gross outrages and mistreatment, but no one will believe you. You will be punished and humbled and greatly confused, and Heaven will seem closed to you, God will seem dead and indifferent, you will try to be recollected, but instead be distracted, you will try to pray and your thoughts will fly, you will seek me fruitlessly and without avail for I shall hide in noise and shadows and I shall seem to withdraw when you need me most. Everyone will seem to abandon you. Confession will seem tedious, Communion stale and unprofitable; you will practice each daily exercise of worship and devotion, but all through necessity, as if you stood outside yourself and hated what you'd become. And yet you will believe, Mariette, but as if you did not believe; you will *always hope, but as if you did not hope; you will love your Savior, but as if you did not love him, because in this time your true feelings will fail you, you will be tired of life and afraid of death, and you will not even have the relief of being able to weep."*

Part 2

Crickets.

Heat.

Something wriggles in the green stew of algae at the water's edge.

High up on a stark jut of wasted hickory, a hoot owl turns its head completely around and persecutes the night with its stare.

Church windows and song. Matins. Lauds. And then footsteps.

Silence.

Wingsoar and a soft thud in the garden, and then a frantic writhing that the whacking wings carry away.

A hawkmoth touches down on the tension of still water, turns on a soft breeze, and unsticks itself. The moonsweep is sliced with ripples.

*   *   *

Seeing herself in a nighted window, a sister holds back her gray hair, then holds her hands tight at her cheeks. She is horrified. She withdraws.

Water drips onto pink brick in the garth.

White skirt, black sandals, castanets.

Written on a rafter is: "They mortify their bodies with abstinence." And on the one just after it: "May they renew and strengthen their souls by good actions."

Electric blue just before sunrise and two white points of light high overhead. The planet Jupiter. The planet Venus.

Guernsey cows trudge toward the milking barn in the English green of timothy grass.

Prime. Warblers, finches, orioles, sparrows, peewees, juncos, robins, blue jays.

Mass of Saint Joachim, Confessor, Husband of
Saint Anne and Father of the Blessed Virgin Mary.

Mixt. Sisters are eating in the Great Silence.

The mistress of novices halts in front of Mariette, whose head is down in prayer. She bluntly raps the wide plank table with the head of her cane and the postulant looks up with surprise. Mother Saint-Raphaël gives her the handsigns, *Terce, you, chapter room*, and Mariette smiles in agreement as she tractably sips her barley tea.

*   *   *

And she is sitting in afflicted repose on a green tapestried footstool while Mother Saint-Raphaël worriedly scowls at Mariette's high school essay about her yearning for a religious life. "We teach a plain style of writing," the mistress of novices says, and shuts the pages inside a manila folder and tosses it onto the floor beside her.

"I hope I haven't displeased you, Mother."

She smiles. "You haven't yet, but you will. With your mistress it is inevitable." Mother Saint-Raphaël sits in a soft Empire chair slightly above the girl and gently touches her white hands together as she says, "I am the former mother superior here."

"I know."

She smiles again. "Of course." She tilts her cane against the wall and tells Mariette, "I have arthritis that acts up sometimes."

"How horrible!"

Mother Saint-Raphaël contemplates the postulant for some time before saying she was in Belgium with their mother general when Mariette first interviewed with the prioress, so she'll now say what she would have then. Which is: "We are here to learn and to love." The mistress of novices stares at her, and goes on, "Your sisters here chose religious life for many different reasons. Some have a natural disposition for it. Some have had a crisis or trial that made the Divinity profoundly real to them and since then have had an overpowering need for daily communion with God. Still others have felt themselves famished and bereft until an accidental experience with our shared affection and prayers unexpectedly revived in them the possibility of joy. Every reason inspired by God is a good one for joining us here."

The girl is following her with flashing eyes and the go-ahead grin of a teacher urging some foolish drudge to try out a faulty idea. Mother Saint-Raphaël asks, "Shall I guess what your own reasons were, Mariette?"

She smiles but doesn't say.

"You grew up with high ambitions in a village where too many girls married young and got pregnant often and aged gruesomely and, after hard use, died. And you thought you were extraordinary. You thought, quite rightly, that it was God who had made you so talented and smart and pretty and ever so much better than the girls who hated you, who never invited you to stay overnight or try on clothes or talk inanities about true love. So you kept to your room and wrote affected poetry and read the books your teachers talked about when you strolled with them in the schoolyard, and you thanked God for your loneliness and intellect, you even thanked Him for your dissatisfactions. You were distressed by attentions and misunderstandings. You were approached by boys and were only baffled. You heard praise and you thought, *Is that truly me?* Everyone talked grandly about your future but when you thought of it, as you *constantly* did, you were just as constantly filled with anguish. And, against your will, you began thinking of the sisters here in their priory, of their aloneness and silence and higher purpose, and soon it seemed the religious life, with all its penance and hardships and imperfections, was freedom for you, and the holy life you'd been seeking all along." She pauses and stares at the postulant, and she asks, "Have my own petty and selfish reasons partly touched yours, Mariette?"

She hints at no irony as she tactfully says, "You have discovered and honored me."

Mother Saint-Raphaël smiles. "Well put," she says, and stands up. She parts the curtains and peers outside at sunshine and the unpainted weatherboarding of the milking barn. "Oh, proud I was, and swelled up with willfulness and self-praise, until God grew irritated with my haughtiness and I heard Christ's words in the gospel of John, saying, '*You* have not chosen Me, but *I* have chosen you, and *ordained* you, that you should go and bring forth *fruit,* and that your fruit should remain.' "

"I have always liked that part," Mariette says.

Mother Saint-Raphaël turns. She pauses until she sees that the girl has heard and understood. "Do not lose your fervor, Mariette. Do not grow bored and dull and disinclined to pray. Do not become again the haughty girl you were, but the holy nun that God wants you to be."

"I shall."

Mother Saint-Raphaël walks to the chapter room door and opens it. Five novices are dallying in the hallway, but quickly tidy themselves when the mistress stares. She says to Mariette, "Sister Saint-Denis is expecting you upstairs in the classroom by the scriptorium. You'll be having religion there at this hour until you take vows."

"What are the seven deadly sins?"

"Excessive pride, anger, covetousness, lust, gluttony, laziness, envy."

"What are the seven healing virtues?"

"Humility, meekness, liberality, chastity, temperance, diligence, sisterly love."

"What are the seven spiritual works of mercy?"

"Correcting sinners, comforting the afflicted, counseling the troubled, forgiving offenses, teaching the ignorant, suffering all wrongs patiently, praying for the living and the dead."

"What are the seven joys of Our Lady?"

"The Annunciation, the Visitation, the Nativity of Our Lord, the Adoration of the Magi, the Finding of the Child Jesus in the Temple, the Apparition of the Risen Christ to His Mother, and the Assumption and Coronation of the Blessed Virgin in Heaven."

"What are the seven charisms?"

"Evangelism, eloquence, healing, prophecy, wisdom, contentment with poverty, true discernment of evil spirits."

"What are the seven sins against the Holy Spirit?"

"There are only six. Despair of salvation, presumption of God's mercy, impugning the Christian faith, hard obstinacy in sin, impenitence at death, and jealously over our sister's blessings and increase in holiness."

"Excellent, Mariette."

Mass of Saint Hyacinth, Confessor.

Work. Mariette kneels on ginger-brown earth as she plants winter seeds in a hot-weather garden that Sister Saint-Luc has harrowed and Sister Saint-Pierre has grooved with a stick. Brussels sprouts, kale, and savory cabbage. Sister Hermance is just behind her with a tin watering can. Sister Saint-Luc sings the hymn "Immaculate Mary" and the sisters join her.

Hot breezes slide through the bluejoint grass. Sister Sabine is walking behind a horse-pulled thresher in the barley field. When Sister Hermance pours, she sees the water puddle like hot cocoa, but soon it is just a faint stain in the earth. Killdeer kite down and dally above Mariette, as if suddenly interested. Turtledoves watch from the telephone wire. And Sister Hermance thinks, *We will have a bounty. Everything she touches will grow. Dirt puts itself in her hands.*

Mass of Saint Agapitus, Martyr.

At collation Sister Pauline is in the high pulpit, continuing their reading from the *Revelations of Divine Love:* " 'We can ask reverently of our lover whatever we will. For by nature our will wants God, and the good will of God wants us. We shall never cease wanting and longing until we possess him in fullness and joy. Then we shall have no further wants.' "

While she reads, Sister Saint-Michel, who is being punished for handsigning in choir, goes up to the professed sisters with a handleless teacup and gives the signs, *Please*, *food*. Everyone denies her except for Sisters Monique and Saint-Estèphe, who sullenly turn teaspoons of onion soup into the penitent's cup, and Mother Saint-Raphaël, who tears off a piece of hot bread. Sister Saint-Michel then curtsies to the prioress and crawls underneath a table to eat. She seems to be near tears.

And so Mariette is surprised at recreation when Sister Saint-Michel plays badminton in the yard with Sisters Zélie, Aimée, and Saint-Estèphe, jumping and shrieking joyously as she tries to hit a high, fluttering shuttlecock.

Mass of Saint Jane Frances de Chantal, Widow.

Ever since one particular extern joined them—God be praised, she is gone now, she makes jellies, she is married to a trapper—Sister Saint-Léon has been humbly required to teach table etiquette to all those who would imitate Our Lady in decorum and *délicatesse*. Even to ones as perfectly refined as the postulant. She therefore sits Mariette at a collation place setting while pointing out how offensive it is to feast beside or across from a sister whose hands and nails seem not to have been cleaned since birth, who imparts a general *stickiness* to everything she touches, whose wholesome food shows itself again and again as she changes it by chewing. Mariette is to seat herself quietly, without heaves and sighs and jostling. She is not to tuck her napkin under her chin, nor use it for unseemly purposes that have nothing at all to do with the fastidious dabbing of the cheeks and lips. She is not to put her knife in her mouth, nor pour coffee or tea in her saucer rather than drinking it from the proper utensil. She is not to reach over another sister for flavorings and butter, nor bumptiously stand up to grab something not near at hand. They are not pigs at a trough here, Sister Saint-Léon says. She is to hold her face at least four inches from her food. And if there are fish bones or cherry pits or foreign things that ought not be swallowed, she is not to spit them obstreperously onto her plate, but softly allow them back onto her spoon and subtly deposit them just beside her servings. And henceforth, Mother General has declared, sucking and smacking noises will not be tolerated. Such *politesse*, Sister Saint-Léon says, can be quite readily acquired, with a firm purpose of amendment, and is really not as difficult as it sounds; it may indeed already be natural to the postulant.

And if not, Mariette says, I shall practice in secret.

Fourteenth Sunday after Pentecost.

Wide milk cows are tearing up green shocks of grass in the pasture. Each chews earnestly, like a slow machine, until the roots disappear in her mouth and she goes back to the grass again.

Hothouse flowers on a sill in a jar. The green shafts seem to break at the water line and get milkier while angling down. Sister Honoré plucks some pink dahlia petals whose withering edges are tanning with age.

Sister Ange is throned upright on stacked pillows and stares outside from an infirmary bed that Sister Marie-Madeleine has slanted up with wood blocks. She worries over the pleasure she takes in viewing the yard, but she thinks it is like a prayer, seeing so many of God's favors and blessings on their priory. She sees Sister Véronique sitting in an Adirondack chair in the shade, sternly peering over half-glasses as she sketches pigeons on the dark green lawn. Externs stand in the yellow wheat as an eastern wind crawls over it. Torn clouds are in slow gait to the south, like a straggle of gray and white house dogs hobbling to their beds. Sister Ange smiles while remembering her childhood, and Comtesse, Galette, Bibi, and Richelieu.

Mass of the Beheading of Saint John the Baptist, and of
Saint Sabina, Martyr.

Père Marriott honors Saint Sabina's martyrdom just before the Epistle and Sister Sabine flushes pink, and just after giving her Holy Communion, the priest rests his hand on the milkmaid's head and murmurs, *"Bon anniversaire."* At the noontime meal Sister Sabine is invited to sit next to the mistress of novices, and she beams as her sister externs present her with husking gloves in honor of her saint, but then blushes hotly when Mother Saint-Raphaël asks her to tell them about Saint Sabina, and only slightly rises to announce, "She was persecuted by Herod."

"Emperor Hadrian," Mother Saint-Raphaël says.

"Excuse me, Mother. Yes."

Mother Saint-Raphaël asks, "Was she a virgin?"

Sister Sabine seems dismayed.

"She was not," Mother Saint-Raphaël says. She turns to the sisters. "She was martyred in Rome in the second century. And she may have been with child."

"Oh dear," Sister Monique says.

Sister Sabine says desperately, "She's told me often in prayer that I do her proud."

Mother Saint-Raphaël smiles and pats her hand.

Alkali water and powdered sodium carbonate are slopped across the kitchen flooring, and a scullery brush that's hard as a horse comb scrubs lard and grease and hard clear stains from the dark brown planks.

Sister Zélie is on all fours with the new postulant when she notices that the harsh ripsaw noise of Mariette's own hard scouring has ceased. She looks to her left and sees the shut-eyed girl kneeling upright on her fingertips and softly praying into the room's emptiness. Sister Zélie watches until Mariette pauses and raises her knees to release her hands and goes back to her work again.

Sister Saint-Léon walks in with dishes and an iron saucepan of knives and walks out again. The extern knocks the floor with the wooden handle of her scrub brush and Mariette looks up. Sister Zélie signs, *Why, under, knees, hands?*

So, not, sin, against, purity.

You, always, pray, so?

The pretty girl hesitates and shows her agreement. *Since, was, child.*

Sister Zélie signs, *Easy, purity, here.* She grins. *Too tired.*

September. Mass of Saint Serapia, Virgin, Martyr.

The skies haze with heat and Mariette and Sister Marie-Madeleine are backing along a green hayfield, snagging down the high grass with dull scythes. Sweat rises on their hands like pinheads. A hide of chaff and dust finds the wetness in their habits. And in the turbulence of hot and brutal effort, Sister Marie-Madeleine huffs and shrieks like a mother in labor pains. And then Sister Marie-Madeleine turns and puts down her scythe as if she's just been called. Mariette stalls in her work and watches as Sister Marie-Madeleine hurries to Mother Céline, half an acre away. She jealously sees them talk, and then sees Sister Marie-Madeleine shroud her face in her hands. She keens and jerks with sobs. Mother Céline holds the nun in her arms and Mariette looks away.

Within a few minutes, Sister Marie-Madeleine is beside Mariette in the green hayfield again.

"Your father?" Mariette asks, and immediately hates her thoughtlessness and childish curiosity.

Sister Marie-Madeleine says, "She recited to me from the psalms. 'Although they go forth weeping, carrying the seed to be sown, they shall come back rejoicing, carrying their sheaves.'" And then Sister Marie-Madeleine goes back to work, attacking the high grass with her scythe.

Compline. Sister Emmanuelle retreats a half-step in her stall so she can peer behind Sister Antoinette and discreetly adore the new postulant in her simple night-black habit and scarf. She's as soft and kind as silk. She's as pretty as affection. Even now, so soon, she prays the psalms distinctly, as if the habit of silence has taught her to cherish speech. And she seems so shrewd, so pure, so prescient. Sister Emmanuelle thinks, *She is who I was meant to be.*

And then the sisters turn and walk out in silence, and Sister Emmanuelle thrills as she hesitates just enough so that Mariette passes by. And then she quickly presses her left hand into the postulant's. Mariette walks ahead and hides her surprise as she secretly glimpses her hand and the gift of Sister Emmanuelle's starched cambric handkerchief with its six-winged seraphim holding a plumed letter *M* gorgeously stitched into it in hours of needlepoint. She gives the seamstress an assessing glance and then Sister Emmanuelle flushes pink as the girl shyly smiles.

Mass of the Most Holy Name of Mary.

Sisters Marthe, Sabine, Saint-Michel, and Claudine stoop among high green cornstalks in husking gloves, adroitly twisting and yanking the sweet-corn ears and tossing them against a tin bangboard on a horse-pulled wagon. Sister Marthe yells out, "Here's one the size of a cubit!" And then there's no sound but that of cornstalks rustling against human movement, and the squeak and tear and tin noise of the harvest.

Evening recreation. Sisters Anne, Virginie, and Marie-Madeleine stand waist-deep in brittle blond cattails by the pond, solemnly watching their bamboo fishing poles and the stick floats that bob and twirl on the stinking water. Henri Marriott walks up and speaks French to Sister Monique. She raises a tin bucket and the old priest stares inside, asking, *"Comment appelez-vous ces poissons en anglaise?"*

"Lunkers," says Sister Marie-Madeleine, and the sisters titter.

14 September 1906

Dear Père Marriott,

I have so much to tell you of Christ's kindnesses and promises to me, but before reading further I plead to you: Do not believe anything I say. Writing you gives me such consolation, but as I begin to put words on paper a great fear overwhelms me. I have such fantastic and foreign things to report that it seems highly likely that I have dreamed them. I shall say it frankly here that my head is a bit strange, for I have seen and heard impossible things, and whenever before has Christ appeared to souls as sinful as mine?

She can see a hundred fireflies out her window. Each is a red dot, then a line, like a pen of red ink crossing a *t*. She goes on writing for half an hour and then stacks the pages before folding them inside a white envelope on which she prints "Confessional Matter." She carries it to the prioress's suite on the way to Compline and hurriedly puts it in the mail slot.

Extracts of an Inquiry into Certain Wonderful Events at the Priory of Our Lady of Sorrows, Having to Do with Mariette

Baptiste, a Youthful Postulant Here, as Carried Out by Reverend Henri Marriott for the Sisters of the Crucifixion, and Faithfully Recorded by Sister Marguerite in the Winter Months of This Year of Our Lord, 1907.

—We are talking now with Sister Philomène.

—Yes, Father.

—And you are how old?

—Twenty-five.

—And you have been here . . . ?

—Three years now. I entered just after my college graduation.

—How were you christened?

—Janet Keating.

—Sister Marguerite is just taking down what we say.

—I see that.

—You should know that she is, for these purposes, no more than a hearing and writing machine. She has promised on pain of excommunication not to whisper a word of these proceedings.

—We know each other well, Father.

—Of course. And you know Mariette just as well?

—Even better.

—How is that?

—She is my friend.

—Have you a particular affection toward her?

—We have rules against that here.

—But were you to meet another sister in the hallway, I presume you'd be a tad happier if that sister turned out to be Mariette?

—I have been very happy here. Even before she came.

—You needn't hide honest feelings from me, Sister Philomène. Your own holiness and obedience are not being discussed here.

—She is my particular friend.

—Well said.

Mass of the Seven Sorrows of the Blessed Virgin Mary.

Sister Philomène and Mariette are working with Sister Agnès in the laundry. Weak rain is easing down the cellar window-panes, and two frail light bulbs hang from green electrical cords woven through the joists overhead. Sister Agnès is at an ironing board while Mariette and Sister Philomène crank rinsed corporals through old hand mangles.

Warm water that smells like grapefruits is sheeting grayly on the rollers as it presses from the wet linen.

Sister Philomène has a prayerbook open on a white cup-board that holds boxes of soap and starches, and she's whispering a novena to Saint Joseph as she turns a green iron wheel. She shows greater effort and then stares with astonishment at the rollers, seeing her white habit somehow caught up in them and rumplingly squeezing through.

Sister Philomène bashfully tugs her habit out before grinning forgivingly at Mariette.

Weeks later Sister Philomène is sitting in formation class with the four other novices while Mother Saint-Raphaël first upbraids them for their tepid essays on spirituality and then invites the postulant to read from an exam that Sister Saint-Denis has just corrected. Each of them hates Mariette as she stands there prettily, shyly, with shaking hands, and reads:

"We know from Church teaching that the soul has no true pleasure but in love. And we know from our experience that extreme bliss can only come from extreme passion. When we unite these ideas, we see how important it is for God to be away from us and be the one we pine for but cannot have, for desiring God invigorates us. Desiring him, but never fully having him, we cannot grow tired or slack. We know the joy of his 'hereness' now and then, but were his distance and indifference all we had, it would still be sufficient if we sought and cherished it.

"Even for the complete and immediate possession of his heart, I would not have passive tranquillity. And so I prize my hours of penance and rapture as the greatest blessings that were ever mine, and I would rather be condemned to know him no more than to know him without feeling the ardor and fervor that his presence inspires."

Mother Saint-Raphaël stops her there and gives Mariette permission to sit with the novices as she takes up the theme of Christ's passion versus theirs. Sister Geneviève is giggling at something Sister Pauline has said, but Sister Philomène leans toward the postulant and whispers, "Will you please let me read that for meditation?"

Mariette smiles and hastily writes slantwise on her exam before she passes it. Sister Philomène reads, "I knew you'd understand," and hides it inside her textbook.

—And you became friendly?

—Yes.

—You knew little about her till then?

—We have no histories here. We try to live wholly in the present, just as God does.

—Yes?

—We talked about our childhoods. She dressed her dolls as Jesus and Mary, just as I did. She played in a habit just like the one that her sister Annie wore. She whipped herself with knotted apron strings. She rebuked temptations against chastity by lying naked on thorns.

—She seems to me quite ordinary.

—Well, that's the point, isn't it?

In November. Sister Philomène has shoved the six great refectory tables against the walls so the floorboards can be scrubbed, and Mariette is with her on her hands and knees, scouring the wood with sand and powdered lime and a pig bristle brush.

Water shines on a floor darkened to a sienna brown and Mariette's black habit and scarf are mirrored as she works.

She is barefoot and her skirt is pinned up as high as her thighs in order to protect the habit's cloth from stain. Faint brown hairs stir on her calves as she moves. Her heels and toes are pink with callus.

She stops scouring with a shocked expression and she hesitantly rises up until she's kneeling there with her hands joined in prayer. Her wet blue eyes are overawed as she stares ahead at a wall and she seems to be listening to something just above her, as a girl might listen to the cooing of pigeons.

Shutting her eyes, she talks voicelessly, with great passion, and opens her hands as priests do at the *pax vobiscum.* And then she swoons as though she's lost herself and has become only her clothes.

—Was she in ecstasy?

—She said so.

—And what else did she tell you?

—She said, "Where was I?" And then she seemed to be recollected and she said Christ had talked to her.

—About what?

—She said she couldn't tell me. She'd been told to hide His words in her heart.

—And it's your opinion that she was speaking the truth.

—Oh yes. I think she's a saint.

Ember Day. Mass of Saint Januarius, Bishop, and
His Companions, Martyrs.

Sister Saint-Estèphe wakes up after an hour's sleep and after
a great deal of restlessness goes to the chandlery. She heats
paraffin wax and stearic acid in a saucepan and then stirs in
a hot mixture of bayberry wax and a purple dye. She prays
the joyful mysteries of the rosary while scouring her candle
molds, then carries the saucepan to an iron trivet on the win-
dowsill and, just after midnight, walks down to the dim oratory to adore Our Lady of Sorrows. She's just getting used
to the church's darkness when she hears the hush of a habit,
and she's surprised to see their postulant kneeling in her
stall.

She handsigns, *Each night, here?*
Yes.
Sleep, when?
Don't.

Mass of Our Lady of Ransom.

Chapter and Compline. Every sister in choir is affectionately
following Reverend Mother Céline as she fluently strolls up
and down the oratory, first giving a short report of interna-
tional events, and then talking about Sister Antoinette's worries for the late-September grape harvest, and going over their
next week's assignments in the winery, grange, hallways, scullery, laundry, milking barn, or orchard. She then gets a church
basket of handwritten notes from Sister Catherine. "We shall
now pray for our petitioners."

Each petition is gradually unfolded and read aloud to
the sisters in order to request their intercession for the health
of a child with impetigo, for a farmer whose faith has left
him, for a hot-blooded girl who's run away, for a mechanic

who's lost half a foot in a steam-powered thresher, for an ill, tired, and friendless widow who's asking God to please let her die. When she has read them all, Mother Céline lowers her head and raises her folded hands to her mouth as though forbidding her own speech. And Mariette thinks, *I have been here forty days and she hasn't talked to me since the first.*

Their mother superior then says, "We shall also pray for one of ours who is undergoing great torment."

Mariette gazes around the oratory. Each nun stares at the prioress in common. Each stares at her separately.

Mass of Saints Isaac Jogues, John de Brebeuf, Charles Garnier, Anthony Daniel, Gabriel Lallemant, Noel Chabanel, John de Lalande, and Rene Goupil, Martyrs.

White clouds travel and infest the horizon. Fruit trees shift their feet like hired hands. Sister Marthe is standing on a paint-spotted ladder inside a pear tree so that her wooden *sabots* alone are unhidden until a great branch cracks away and her ripsaw flashes silver in the sun.

Mother Saint-Raphaël is hoeing weeds around a garden bench as Mariette kneels with pruning shears and snips back the wood canes on pink rosebushes. Sister Claudine is fifteen yards away as she heaves and shakes ammonium sulfate onto a tilled flower bed. Every now and then she pauses and stares at the postulant with envy. Why, Mariette cannot understand, for Mother Saint-Raphaël hoes in silence. Even when Mariette chats about trifles and foolishness, she sees the mistress of novices frowning at her, as if trying to find a hidden character behind the girl's eyes. And Mother Saint-Raphaël only sighs when Mariette talks about religion.

She is surprised, therefore, when she pricks the heel of her hand with a thorn and irritatedly presses up a bead of blood, and Mother Saint-Raphaël interestedly kneels opposite her and holds Mariette's hand in both her own. "Oh my dear," she says. "Are you badly hurt?"

"Oh no; just a thorn."

"Shall I get something for it?"

"I'll be fine, truly."

Mother Saint-Raphaël puts spit onto her forefinger and softly caresses the blood from the wound, and there's such an odd confusion of feelings in the grandmotherly face that Mariette hesitantly wrests her hand away.

Everything changes in Mother Saint-Raphaël then, as if a great door has slammed shut inside her. "Don't misinterpret simple tenderness," she says.

Mariette travels between worry and sympathy before she replies in humility, "I have, Mother. I see that now."

Mother Saint-Raphaël gets up with effort and goes back to work and hoes with a kind of urgency. And when, just before meditation, she walks with Mariette to the tool room, she says, "There's a great deal about you that troubles me."

Mass of the Dedication of the Basilica
of Saint Michael the Archangel.

Walking into the oratory for Prime, Sister Léocadie holds her stomach and whispers to Sister Pauline, "I have cramps." And at the pause before the reading she faints, wrenching and hurting the pew in her slow heavy fall. Every nun stays as she was until Mariette anxiously lays down her Psalter and gets up from her stall.

Sister Léocadie is paper-white and woozily slumped against the pew, but she pulls away in horror when the postulant tries to help her, hissing, "Don't, Sister! The mistress!"

Mother Saint-Raphaël takes four steps out onto the oratory floor and scowls at Mariette and then Sister Léocadie until the ill novice kneels upright again. Mother Saint-Raphaël then pettishly withdraws to her place in the choir.

Sister Léocadie is punished at Mixt by being ordered to prostrate herself on the floor as if she's been nailed facedown on a crucifix. The sisters hesitate only to inchingly lift up their skirts before stepping over her. When it is Mariette's turn, however, Sister Léocadie senses her halting and slowly descending to the floor and joining her on the cross beside her. And Mariette stays like that, simply praying, until Mixt has ended.

—Was anything said, Sister Léocadie?

—Yes; I told Mariette she'd go hungry now. She just answered that she'd had Christ's body at Mass and that was food enough.

—Was she trying to impress you with her piety?

—I don't think she thinks about it.

October 2nd. Mass of the Holy Guardian Angels.

Horses shamble lazily up a knoll and browse the grass near their hooves.

The skies are gray as habits and all the greens are darkening with a faint and chilling mist.

Twenty-six nuns are hunching along the grapevines in their *sabots* and jean aprons and dusters, snapping grape bunches from their stems and skidding wide French baskets along or teaming on the handles to tiltingly carry them to the pig wagons on the roadway.

The psalms of Terce and Sext are recited in the vineyard and the sisters pray the Angelus while slouching tiredly in to dinner. Work replaces Méridienne and classes, Nones are read privately by the water tank, and the grapes are crushed just before Vespers, Sisters Aimée, Virginie, Marthe, Félicité, and Mariette tying their habits as high as their thighs and getting up into the great oaken vats to walk and trounce and slop in the oozing grape juice and skins. And then the prioress humbly walks out to them with plush white towels and a copper verrière, and she kneels before the sisters who have trodden the grapes as she gently washes their feet.

Mass of Saint Francis of Assisi, Confessor.

Class. Waving her hand eraser over the blackboard like a fat farmboy in wild hurrah, Sister Saint-Denis gets rid of her drawing of the Great Chain of Being and then tries to think what she can say to use up the five minutes until Sext. Were her habit red and she bearded white, Sister Saint-Denis could play Santa Claus. She merrily smiles at Mariette and asks, "Are you still liking our convent?"

"Oh yes, Sister."

"We are like the tides here. We come and go. We don't hurry; we don't worry; we try not to wrestle too much with our inner torments and petty irritations."

Shutting her textbook on a pencil, Mariette glances up. "Have there been complaints about me?"

Sister Saint-Denis gives it some thought before saying, "You haven't been mentioned." White checks shine in dark eyes rich as plums. "Which is not such a good thing outside, but here in Our Lady of Sorrows is not so very bad."

"I have to learn that."

Sister Saint-Denis says, "Ever since I have grown older, I have forgotten all my hard penances and fasting and have given particular attention to our Redeemer, in whose presence we live. And I have realized how much simpler it is to pray and keep united with God when I see Him as the source and sum of everything I do. When I walk, I owe it to God that I still can. When I sleep, it is with His permission. My breathing, my happiness, even my being a woman—all are His gifts to me. So it is my prime intention that whenever I do these practical things, they will be contemplative acts of praise and thanksgiving repeated over and over again. Even when it seems impossible to believe that some pain or misery is from God, I try to believe it and thank Him for it. You should try such a prayer, Mariette."

    —And she said she'd try?

    —She said she didn't have the patience for it.

    —Meaning what?

    —Well, I presume she meant she's too zealous. She meant she's still infatuated with our sisterhood. Even our worst penances are too easy for her. Hundreds of postulants have been that way at times.

    —And so, you do not find her fanatical?

    —Christ shines from her. She is Christian perfection. She is lovely in every way.

Mass of Saint Bridget, Widow.

Hard white sunshine heating the frost, and the blue sky high and wide behind iron-gray trees tattered by golden leaves. The hills are tan and rose and magenta. Chimney swifts toss and play in the air. Sister Anne and Sister Agnès heave heavy avalanches of wash onto a gray wool blanket and then go inside for more, and Mariette hangs sweet wet sheets on the clotheslines until she is curtained and roomed by them.

Sister Agnès slinks through a gap in the whiteness with a straw basket of underthings that they silently pin up in the hidden world inside the tutting, luffing, campaigning sheets.

Half an hour passes. Wind tears at their work. Sister Agnès aches from reaching. She blows the sting from her reddened fingers. She watches the postulant as the tilting sheets wrap around her and shape her. She watches the girl as she tenderly releases herself, as though tugging a ghost's hands away.

Nineteenth Sunday after Pentecost.

Mariette goes to the scriptorium with Sister Hermance, Léocadie, and Pauline after Sunday Nones but is intrigued into an hour of talk about mystical theology with Sister Marguerite and cannot get away. She sees the novices try to disappear within the peach sunlight at the great table, reading sixteenth-century books with hard pages that turn with a tearing sound. And underneath that she hears the librarian going on and on about the Desert Fathers.

And then she abandons herself to God's will and hears Sister Marguerite teaching her, "When Saint John of the Cross prayed before the crucifix, Our Lord is supposed to have asked Him, 'Dear John, what will you have from Me in return for the service you have done Me?' Unhesitatingly, that great saint replied that he wanted 'naught but suffering and to be despised for Your sake.' "

"Yes."

"Excuse me?"

"I, too, have prayed for that."

Sister Marguerite heatedly stares and says with intensity, "I have been boring you, haven't I." She angrily goes to the wooden card catalog and squints at her own handwriting there until the novices get up and hurry out.

"Sister, I'm sorry. I had no intention—"

Sister Marguerite interrupts the postulant by nastily smiling and saying, "We all have intentions, Mariette. Even if we don't understand them. And you, my dear sweet child, are a flirt."

Mass of Saint Teresa of Avila, Virgin.

She uses hot pads as she heaves a sloshing tin washtub along a kitchen aisle to the table where Sister Hermance is stacking the saucers and milk bowls from Mixt. "We have no more soap," Sister Hermance whispers.

Mariette does not speak. She is peering down at the gray waltz of steam and the air bubbles quivering up from the scorched tin bottom. She looks left and ascertains that Sister Hermance is licking a spoon of pastry batter as she counts the soup bowls in the dish cupboard.

Mariette prays for sorrow and contrition as she turns up her black sleeves and pauses. She then sinks her hands into the penance of hot water, pressing them down to the tin until her palms scald. She winces with pain as she prays.

Sister Hermance heavily nudges into her as she gathers up Mariette's reddened hands. "Enough," she says. She tenderly blows on Mariette's palms like a nursemaid and softly pets them with a stick of butter. "Were you thinking of the souls in purgatory?"

Mariette turns away from her. "I just wanted to hurt."

Mass of Saint Ursula and Companions, Virgins, Martyrs.

Wrens are cheeping wildly and flying from branch to branch in the junipers.

Winter is still just a hint of purple and gold in the hilltop maples. High above them there is a faint sickle moon and twilight skies of indigo blue fading to beryl and green at the treeline.

Sister Dominique strolls in the garth at collation. She hears words from *The Imitation of Christ*. Wisps of smoke unwrap from the stovepipe. She rolls pebbles in her hand.

Workhorses noisily slurp water from a tank and simultaneously pause. Ears twitching, a pregnant mare raises her nose and sniffs the wind in two directions. Her tail flicks and the horses drink again.

Sister Monique. Sister Saint-Léon. Sister Emmanuelle. Walking in the Gethsemani garden. Wincing and smiling at talk of infants.

Star. Another there. And there.

Compline and dismissal.

Mariette gets into her nightgown and kneels on the floor to hastily pen another letter, her hand moving with great speed and urgency across the page.

21 October 1906

> *Either they think that I have been false and dissembling and too good to be true, or they think that I have been so blessed by Our Lord that I am hardly human, that Christ has rewarded this postulant with perfect bliss.*
>
> *Well, it is not always so for me. The hardness and loneliness of our sisterhood possess me when I am least prepared to chase the ill-feelings from me with prayer. Weeks have passed since I have experienced the sweetness of Christ in Holy Communion. Every joy and consolation of the Church has disappeared like jewels dropped from my*

hand into snow. Temptations that never troubled me in the world have now been bestowed on me by Satan in this holiest of places. Sins from my past rise up to haunt me and remind me of my pettiness and weakness so that it seems God could have only utter hatred and contempt for me.

My soul has become a black house furnished in sorrow and pity. I have been dreaming, it seems, a twelve-year dream which has left me tired and weary. What has happened to me, Père Marriott? Where are the holy graces and consolations that brought me into religious life? And where is Jesus? He comes no more when I call to him. I seek him in vain; he answers my questions no more. I shall always love him, of course, but I fear that I shall never again dwell in his love, and I know that I cannot live without him.

She puts down her fountain pen and looks over her pages, holding her knees to her chest in a fetal position just outside the yellow sphere of candlelight. The hiss of her prayers is the only sound.

Mass of Saint Mary Salome.

—We'll speak in French if you like.

—English would be hard for me.

—Sister Marguerite will translate this later. We will start with your name, please.

—Sister Catherine. Earlier I was known as Simone DuBois, from Perpignan. I hardly remember her now. Is there still a Perpignan accent?

—I have not the ear for it. I have been too long in America.

—Even so we French.

—Have you been in this country long?

—With the great indulgence and grace of God, I have been in this priory for forty-seven years. Forty-seven. Yes, and you are so kind to look surprised! Well, I have come to tell you, Father, that this year, or at least these past few months, whenever that holy girl joined us here, have been the most magnificent in my religious life. We are being showered with blessings. And she is the cause. Mariette.

She is working in the priest's sacristy after Terce, washing a great wall of leaded window glass with vinegar as Sister Catherine polishes a golden ciborium and paten and pyx and Père Marriott's own chalice, with its agates and emeralds and sapphires.

Sister Catherine is so hunched she can hardly see ahead and her frail yellow fingers are awry on her hands like hinges hammered from a door. And yet she touches the vessels with tenderness and joy and is humming the "*Tantum Ergo*" to herself as she scours the intricate sunrays of the holy monstrance.

Wringing a sponge, Mariette flinches with sudden pain and bewilderingly heeds her hands.

"Have you hurt yourself?" Sister Catherine asks.

She grins at the aged woman and says, "What a great favor Christ shall be giving me!" And then she soothes her reddened palms with short tastes of her tongue.

—She didn't explain.
—She didn't need to, did she.
—Go on, please.

She and Mariette are strolling in the chestnut grove at Mèridienne. Tan leaves thrash from their sandals. A high tree branch suddenly breaks and shatters its way to the ground. Sister Catherine talks about being homesick for France. She talks affectionately about Edouard, her older brother, who is twenty years dead now, but who once painted wonderfully, in the manner of Jules Breton.

And Mariette tells Sister Catherine about the prioress as she was before she entered the convent. "Each night Annie would join me in my upstairs room for hours at a time! We prayed together, we talked about Christ's great affection for all humanity, and how I should have an intense horror for sin. With Annie I first found myself before Jesus crucified. Oh, to see it, Sister Catherine! Such blood flowed from his hands and head! And he was having such trouble breathing! We watched in tears, Annie and I, and she told me, 'Look, Mariette, and learn how one loves.' And she said, 'Jesus has given himself wholly to you. Will you give yourself wholly to him?' Yes, I told her; yes and yes a hundred times. And then Annie tenderly petted my hair and told me to be consoled because my sorrow had killed Christ's pain."

—She seemed sensible to you?
—Oh yes; always.
—She gave you the impression that Christ was actually there in her upstairs room?
—She did not make it seem imaginary.
—I have here a letter from Mariette. Shall I read it to you?
—With her permission.
—We have it. She has dated it October 23rd. "Dear Père Marriott," she writes. "Is it possible that I still live, or have I perished all unaware? Of my happiness please speak to me—I have no memory of it. I have only the horrible pain of seeking Jesus and hearing no reply, of having been turned away and repulsed. And yet I think of Christ incessantly, with heartache and terrible yearning, but it is now all so different. What desolations and aridity I now endure in my Masses and my prayers! I do not seem to like them anymore. Hours in the oratory now seem so long and tedious. Each of my meditations is a torture in which everything that was once so tenderly given to me is now teasingly withheld. And

yet I persist. I have not shortened my prayers nor softened my penances, no, in spite of it all I mean to increase them in the hope that this hell on earth will pass. Oh, what have I come to? The sheer insanity of love has never been worse than this." Well, I'll stop there.

—She is passionate. She is perhaps too proud. She is *not* hysterical.

Mass of Saint Raphael, Archangel.

Sister Geneviève hesitates before she begins her dinner reading from *The Imitation of Christ,* and then Mariette stands and she smiles as Sister Hermance chimes a full water glass with her fork. Everyone turns.

"With Michael and Gabriel," Mariette states, "Saint Raphael is one of just three archangels talked about in the Holy Bible. His name in Hebrew means 'God has healed.' Archangel Raphael was the one who told the boy Tobias that he could cure his father's blindness with a fish's gall, and he is associated with the healing waters at the Sheep Pool in Jerusalem, featured in the fifth chapter of John. We honor today the healing powers of our own Mother Saint-Raphaël, knowing that the great archangel speaks through her whenever she forms or corrects us."

Mariette then humbly sits and looks askance at the mistress of novices, who is staring ahead into the great room as if she hasn't heard.

Mass of Saints Chrysanthus and Daria, Martyrs.

Mother Céline cannot sleep, so she handles financial transactions until their first rising when she hears the sexton pass down the hallway to the room of the externs and hears Mariette softly waking them for Matins. And Mother Céline is putting the green account book away when she sees a white envelope fall through the mail slot. She gets it and recognizes the handwriting in the address to their priest.

While she prepares a book of psalms for the first reading, Mother Céline argues with herself about honoring the letter, but she finally opens her sister's "Confessional Matter" just as she's done before, and she frowns as she reads the first paragraph, the fourth, and the fifth. She thinks, *She's impossible. She's too many people. She's too many shades and meanings. She'll only do herself harm.*

She goes to an upper desk drawer and lifts out a flame-red box that once contained a *Missa Romanum.* Eighteen pages are already in it. And now there are two more.

Twenty-first Sunday after Pentecost.
In honor of Christ the King.

Sister Honoré polishes the fall board on the grand piano and looks out a haustus room window at northern winds and storm clouds in ferment and their postulant happily wading in a purple flow of maple leaves. Mariette stoops and puts her hand down in them and they froth up to her chin like sudden pets. Sisters Pauline and Geneviève join Mariette as Sister Honoré sits on the piano bench. She hears their high giggles and hectic talk as she plays one measure of a Chopin étude and steps on the damper pedal.

November 1st. Feast of All Saints.

Mariette gets into Sister Félicité's cardigan sweater at Méridienne and joins Sister Antoinette in the winery's underground cellar, helping her funnel and rack the still-young wines from one oaken barrel to another, and fining the dark lees and tarry sludge from some aging red wines with slowly wandering egg whites. Sister Antoinette then holds a high-shouldered bottle over a frail candle flame as she tenderly pours a *grand cru* vintage into her silver tasting cup. Mariette sniffs it as Sister Antoinette tells her to find there hints of black currants, vanilla, and green cigars.

"Even now it's growing," Sister Antoinette says. "Like our love for God." She holds up the green bottle and points to the dark sediment gradually easing down the side. "And this is?" she asks.

"Our love for ourselves."

Sister Antoinette smiles. "You *are* a clever girl."

All Souls' Day.

Mother Céline is hustling down the hallway toward the visitor's parlor and halting here and there for Mariette, who walks without hurry and with great trepidation, as if this is punishment.

Dr. Baptiste is hulking behind the iron grille in a handsome Kashmir overcoat, an inch of Murad cigarette held inside his hand and grayly hazing the room with its reek. "*Bonjour*, Annie," he gaily says. "*Bonjour*, Mariette." He holds his right palm flat to the grille between them, and Mother Céline meets it with her own while Mariette sits down on a green tapestried chair.

Their father tells them both about the house, his patients, the great canal that is being built on the Isthmus of Panama, a book of tales by O. Henry that he is enjoying, about the Chicago White Sox beating the Chicago Cubs in the third annual World Series, that he is voting for Charles Evans Hughes for governor of New York. Mother Céline kindly acts as if it's all interesting and highly relevant, but Mariette is silent for half an hour, hardly listening to his words, just the fathering thunder of his voice. She truly loves and misses him but she cannot say it. Even looking up from the floor gives her pain, for he is so frontally there, so forceful and huge and masculine. She remembers his first morning coughs, the hollandaise sauce he'd put on her poached eggs, the iodine odor he filled the dining room with, his whistling, his tenderness, the whiskers that nettled her cheek.

She hears him ask, "And you, Mariette? Are you liking the convent?"

"Yes."

"You like it well or just a little?"

Mariette thinks, *Every knife in his house has a keen edge. Every question has just one answer. Every fortune, he says, is finally squandered.* And so she tells him, "I have found happiness here."

"How?"

"We pray. We study. I have always liked that. And everything is very clean."

She hates the hurt she's put in his face but she can think of nothing more that he would understand. She shies a little from his stare and her father turns to Annie and says, "She used to speak for hours and hours to me."

"We have a habit of silence here."

Dr. Baptiste gets up and gingerly adjusts his hat on his head. "Are you going to send her to college?"

"Yes, I think so. If she stays."

"*Are* you staying?" he asks Mariette.

But it's her mother superior who replies, "We have time yet to decide."

Mass of the Four Crowned Martyrs.

Sister Hermance walks the hallway with Sister Marthe and in hushed tones she says she and Mariette were reading epistles in the scriptorium just before Sext when a horrible cat jumped down from a book stack and spurted this way and that around the room as if he were being chased. And Mariette simply stared at him as if that weren't surprising at all. And when the horrible thing sprang up onto Mariette's book and arched his back and hissed at her, Mariette smiled at Sister Hermance and told her not to be frightened, that he was just a hateful demon trying to annoy them. She then got up and opened the scriptorium's door and harshly commanded him, and the humiliated cat skulked out.

Sister Marthe frowns scornfully. "Oh, good gracious, Sister Hermance."

But she insists, "She has powers."

Mass of Saint Gertrude, Virgin.

The sisters are having their noon meal of a flavorless green soup of old garden vegetables, quarter-rounds of steamed rye bread, and a good red wine from Saint-Émilion that hasn't traveled well.

Sister Saint-Stanislas wipes out her soup bowl with her little finger and sucks hard on it, then scrapes her hand along the stained tablecloth and presses up the rye crumbs and licks them from her palm.

Sister Zélie has been assigned the *Lectio Divina* from *The Rule of Saint Augustine*. She reads: " 'From time to time the necessity of keeping order may compel you to use harsh words to the young people who have not yet reached adulthood, in order to keep them in line. In that case you are not required to apologize, even though you yourself consider that you have gone too far. For if you are too humble and submissive in your conduct towards these young people, then your authority, which they should be ready to accept, will be undermined. In such cases you should ask forgiveness from the Lord of all, who knows with what deep affection you love your sisters, even those you might happen to have reproved with undue severity. Do not let your love for one another remain caught up in self-love; rather, such love must be guided by the Spirit.' "

Mariette carries out a tan pitcher from the kitchen and gracefully walks around, topping up water glasses. Sister Saint-Estèphe taps Mariette's upper arm. She gives the hand-signs, *Here, three, months?*

Mariette smiles.

Sister Saint-Pierre handsigns, *We, happy*. And Sister Ange agrees.

Mass of Saint Gregory, Wonderworker, Bishop, Confessor.

Mariette stands in the hallway in front of the confessional, rehearsing her sins behind four other sisters, until she's finally alone and just outside the door and Sister Virginie cringes out. Mariette takes a breath then and walks inside, taking care to firmly shut the door before getting down on the kneeler before the iron grille and purple silk curtain. She makes the sign of the cross and, as she hears Père Marriott blessing her in Latin, she says in English, "Bless, me, Father, for I have sinned since my last confession, one week ago."

"Yes?"

"I have been too easily distracted from hearing the *Lectio*."

"When?"

"At collation yesterday and again at Mixt today."

The priest says nothing. She smells beeswax on the hand-rest and a hint of horse sweat and hours-old tobacco smoke from his side of the confessional.

She confesses that at Saturday's recreation she tried to be entertaining by doing unkind imitations of her religion teacher, the choirmistress, and the mistress of novices. Even through the purple curtain she can see Père Marriott secretly grinning while possibly imagining the slow truckling walk of Sister Saint-Denis, Sister Honoré holding her food near her mouth before suddenly attacking it, the tired sighs and pompous, operatic scorn of Mother Saint-Raphaël.

"Each has some authority over you. Each is your teacher in some way, is she not?"

"Each was easy to do."

"Well, it is a great temptation in communities. You were probably very amusing. Yes, but you must try to think of these imitations as a kind of disobedience. And just imagine how it hurts Jesus to see you making fun of these holy women that He loves so dearly."

"Yes, Father. I shall."

"And your other sins?"

She hesitates for a moment, and then tells him, "I have not been getting consolations from the Mass. I have too little faith or fervor. I feel almost forsaken by God. Spiritually dry."

Père Marriott sighs. "We hear this from the holiest people. Even as far back as Isaiah we read, 'Truly, you are a hidden God.' Even Jesus at his death cried out, '*Eli, Eli, lama sabachthani?*' My God, my God, why have you forsaken me? We have to be patient at times. We must permit God to rest in our presence. We have to believe that our good God not only loves us but is that which is most *intimate* to us. And if we truly need Him, there He'll be. We can always rely on that."

"*Merci bien,* Père Marriott."

"Was there anything else?"

She shakes her head.

Père Marriott assigns the postulant the Litany of the Saints as a penance and then blesses her and absolves her of her sins. And when she is going out, he asks, "Are you writing down your thoughts for me, Mariette?"

She turns to him in surprise but doesn't say.

"Even the prioress has heard about it. Eventually I shall expect to see some pages."

"Soon perhaps," she says.

She writes on a half-sheet of paper, "I have to talk to you!" and she puts it by Mother Céline's water glass at collation. She sees the prioress read it and think about it and hide the note in her gray habit pocket, and then she sees the prioress smile as Sister Saint-Michel serves her.

Twenty-fourth Sunday after Pentecost.

Evening recreation and milking stools in the haustus room. Sister Hermance is fashioning straw dolls; Sister Léocadie is jotting "All is well" on six postcards she's yet to address; Sister Philomène is painting a wholly imaginary Bethlehem of high blue mountains and great waterfalls above a green sward that she's whitely splotched with sheep. Sister Léocadie appraises it and says, "Sister Véronique will hate that."

"I haven't finished."

"She'll hate it more when you do."

And then Sister Pauline shyly walks in from the hallway and says, "We've written a playlet. From the Bible. Shall we perform it for you?"

Sister Philomène puts down her paintbrush and says, "Yes, please."

"Which?" asks Sister Léocadie.

Sister Pauline impishly smiles and whispers, "The Song of Songs."

"Oh, I like that part," Sister Hermance says.

Sister Pauline gently pulls the haustus room door and Mariette is glamorously there, her great dark mane of hair in massacre like the siren pictures of Sheba. She's taken her

habit and sandals off and shockingly dressed her soft nakedness in a string necklace of white buttons that are meant to
seem pearls and red taffeta robe that is like a bloodstain on
linen. The sisters hush as she lounges inside and pinches out
some candlewicks and lazily yawns and seems to gaze yearn-
ingly over their heads to a foreign country.

And then Sister Geneviève stands in the doorway
in her habit but without her veil or cincture or rosary, and
with a white bathtowel wildly turbaned around her head.
She's penciled in a dark mustache that Sister Pauline giggles
at, but Sister Geneviève seems romantically serious and pining as she plays the Bridegroom and recites: "You ravish my
heart, my sister, my promised bride, you ravish my heart
with a single one of your glances, with a single pearl of your
necklace. What spells lie in your love, my sister, my promised bride! How delicious is your love, more delicious than
wine! How fragrant your perfumes, more fragrant than all
other spices! Your lips, my promised one, distilled wild
honey. Honey and milk are under your tongue; and the
scent of your garments is like the scent of Lebanon."

"We shouldn't be doing this," Sister Philomène says, but
no one pays her the slightest attention.

Sister Geneviève walks in.

Mariette turns to the tall windows and widens her arms as
she says in the bride's part: "Awake, O north wind, come,
wind of the south! Breathe over my garden, that its spices may
flow out. Let my Beloved come into his garden, let him taste
its precious fruits."

Sister Philomène is nudged with gusto by Sister Hermance, but she doesn't give back the tiniest glance. She thinks
how Hermance will be big-eyed; she'll make a great O of her
mouth. "Wink, wink," Sister Philomène says.

Mariette wearily and despairingly lies down but holds her
hands in prayer underneath her chin, and there is a pause

until Sister Pauline narrates: "She sleeps, but her heart keeps vigil. And then she hears her Beloved knocking."

Sister Geneviève exaggerates a manly register in order to say: "Open to me, my sister, my love, my dove, my undefiled, for my manly head is damp with dew, my manly locks with the drops of the night."

Mariette pretends sweet temptation as she sits up and puts a hand to her breast and shakenly recites: "I have taken off my tunic, shall I then put it on? I have washed my feet, shall I then soil them?"

"Oh, go ahead," says Sister Léocadie. "Just let him in and get on with it."

Sister Philomène holds her hands to her ears, but Sister Hermance squeals with joy.

Mariette gets up as she says: "My Beloved thrust his hand through the opening, and my heart pounded within me, and I trembled and grew faint when he spoke." She pretends to pause at a door and peeks out. Sister Geneviève is opposite her. Mariette recites: "I rose up to open to my Beloved, with my hands dripping myrrh, pure myrrh dripping off my fingers and upon the handle of the bolt." She hesitates, and Sister Geneviève ever so slowly withdraws and turns. Mariette then recites: "When at last I opened to my Beloved, he had departed and disappeared! My soul failed at his flight." She scurries right and then left while saying: "I sought him but I did not find him, I called to him but he did not answer me." And she then hides behind her hands. "The gatekeepers discovered me as they made their rounds in the City. They beat me, they hurt me, they took away my habit, they who guard the City ramparts."

"How frustrating!" says Sister Léocadie.

While Sister Geneviève goes out the door, Mariette directly addresses her audience, saying: "Oh please, I adjure you, my dearest sisters, O daughters of Jerusalem, if you should ever find my Beloved, what shall you tell him . . . ? That I am sick with love."

And then she gets to her knees below Christ on the crucifix, and one by one the novices get to their knees, too.

Mass of the Presentation of the Blessed Virgin Mary.

Evening. Compline. And then Conference.

Each sister keeps to her seat in the choir pews and concentrates on her just-touching knees or the pink and spotted backs of her hands as she recollects her sins. Foot marries foot in the night's flooding cold.

Wind, and a sigh in the rusting trees just outside the high windows.

Sister Saint-Léon fixes significant effort on pleating a sleeve with fierce pinches.

Sister Agnès tears at a cuticle with her nails. She then irritatedly uses her teeth and sees Mother Saint-Raphaël scowl.

Mariette looks up at the tallow candles overhead. She can hear the wicks hiss as they slowly burn down; she can see a red ash detach itself and float up in a twist of gray smoke. In the tropics, she's heard, there are parrots that are as bright blue as some parts of a flame.

Sister Saint-Pierre coughs and coughs again.

Sister Geneviève heaves her great weight onto one thigh and then gets heavily down on her kneeler. She kisses her rosary's crucifix and pats her forehead and shoulders with a sign of the cross as she says, "Dear God, I humbly ask Your pardon for my sins against You and Your holy Church. And I also beg forgiveness of you, my sisters, for I accuse myself of having committed these wrongs: I have walked too loudly in our hallways and kitchen and have made far too much noise in shutting our doors."

She bows her head as she awaits the judgment of the sisters, but she hears only silence until Sister Dominique agrees by saying, "She has been most conspicuous this past week," and some of the sisters giggle.

Eyes tightly shut, Reverend Mother Céline stands at the oaken grille and softly gives praise to the Holy Spirit, touching her joined knuckles with her mouth. She accepts the silence for half a minute and says, "Will someone else help our sister?"

Everyone is still.

Sister Geneviève looks up and says, "Having heard these accusations, my sisters, I beg that you give me a penance."

The prioress gives it some thought and says, "Sister Geneviève, you are assigned the task of waking us up from our sleep for the next few days, that your noise may be put to holy purpose."

Sister Geneviève gets up from the kneeler and sits, slinging herself against the pew back so heavily that the nails squawk in the wood.

And then the sisters give themselves to their own recollections again.

Sister Sabine scratches her shin until it pinks.

Sister Dominique kneels in order to confess halfheartedness and tedium in her late-night meditations on the Five Precious Wounds.

Sister Saint-Léon, Sister Dominique's associate in the kitchen, says to her, "Every moment this evening I, too, have discovered a hundred defects in my own religious devotions. In your penance, Sister Dominique, please do commend me to Our Lord Jesus, that our shared sins and worthlessness shall not be cause for His just condemnation."

"And so," Sister Dominique acidly says, "you have undervalued even my sins. Even in my confession you selfishly turned our attentions toward Sister Saint-Léon."

She is about to say more but Mother Céline tells her, "You may sit, Sister Dominique."

She does, and five minutes pass.

Sister Catherine sleeps.

Sister Marie-Madeleine skates her right palm along the pew railing and interestedly presses her thumb on a nailhead.

Sister Pauline and Sister Saint-Stanislas trade snickers at hearing the patter of a kitten in full gallop down the hallway.

Mariette then tilts forward onto her own kneeler, kisses her crucifix, and crosses herself. "Dear God, I humbly ask your pardon for my sins against you and your holy Church. And I also beg forgiveness of you, my sisters, for I accuse myself of having committed these wrongs: I have given my eyes great liberty and sought to have my sister join me in foolishness and girlish play."

Sister Saint-Denis asks, "And have you spoken when you should not speak?"

Mariette says, "I have accused myself only of being a great hindrance to prayer."

Sister Félicité is sitting in jury one row behind Mariette. She says, "While I have enjoyed our sister's humor, she is, at times, distracting."

Sister Ange is scratching up the wax on the railing wood as she says, "She is a daily temptation to intimacies and particular attachments."

Sister Saint-Pierre coughs again and again and then she daintily spits into a dinner napkin that she's been keeping under her sleeve.

Sister Saint-Luc is tapping her prayerbook as she now and then hums.

"She's provoked me," Sister Marguerite says, but she does not further explain herself.

A gray-and-white-patched cat is up on the joists overhead, staring down with hazel eyes and slowly lashing its tail.

The prioress asks, "Will someone else help our sister on her way to Christian perfection?"

Mother Saint-Raphaël is as aslant as a roof, her affliction and huff only slightly hidden underneath her hand. She sighs grandly and says, "Our postulant has been too proud. She has been a princess of vanities. She has sought our admiration and attention in a hundred ways since she has joined our convent. She hopes we will praise her for being pretty and fetching and young. She is slack in her work and lax in her conscience. She has been a temptation to the novices and a pet to all the professed sisters. Ever since I have been her mistress, she has been a snare and a worldliness to me and a terrible impediment to the peace and interests of the Holy Spirit."

Hearing her own passion and antipathy, Mother Saint-Raphaël pauses and adds, "I know that I myself have been guilty of these faults and a hundred others, for which I, too, humbly ask God's pardon."

Even the professed nuns are sitting there in astonishment.

Sister Geneviève angles back in order to gaze at Mother Saint-Raphaël.

Mariette is being hunted with the hawking eyes of the others.

The prioress says nothing for a minute and then asks, "Will someone else help Mademoiselle Baptiste on the hard path toward her simple vows?"

Mariette hears only quiet.

Embarrassed and distressed, Mariette raises up a little and says in a trembling voice, "Having heard these accusations, my sisters, I beg that you give me a penance."

The prioress says, "Mother Saint-Raphaël?"

She is sitting as she was, but now her iron-gray eyes stare at Mariette as she says, "When you next recite your rosary, I would recommend that you ask for some sign that you truly have a religious calling. And please meditate upon the pain and sorrows of Our Lord. Especially His agony in the garden, His scourging at the pillar, His being crowned with a garland of thorns."

She stands in her white-painted room, seeing no moon, in a sour nightgown that itches, on floor planks that are keen as iron against the skin of her feet. She loses one word of a prayer and then she loses another. She begins again and forgets that she's begun. She thinks she's gotten through the Annunciation and so she says to herself, "The second joyful mystery: the Visitation."

And then she sags against the gray stone sill of the window casing and twists away from the night outside, tenderly holding her sore right breast as if she's just discovered it.

She skids down the wall until she's squatting in the night of the room.

Twenty-fifth Sunday after Pentecost.

Compline. She prays without thought. Without emotion. She is a book without words or pictures. She is a night without moon.

Mass of Saint Sylvester, Abbot.

Sleep get up pray pray pray pray pray pray pray.

Mass of Saint Saturninus, Martyr.

Mariette is slowly walking the great dining hall with a jeroboam of straw-white wine at dinner, when Mother Saint-Raphaël belatedly arrives, spiking her crooked cane on the floor planks and sitting down with the great weight of old age. She scowls at the five novices and then at Mariette and taps her knuckles on the ironed tablecloth in order to beckon the postulant over.

Mariette cradles the jeroboam as she obeys, crouching by the refectory table so that Mother Saint-Raphaël can talk confidingly. She whispers, "We two shall dispense with silence."

"Yes, Mistress."

"Mother Céline is ill. You are to take a hot pot of tea to Reverend Mother, and you will please put in it three teaspoons of this wild senna." She gives Mariette a white slip of paper that she's rolled and twisted shut at both ends. "She will be purged of her pernicious humors and the great vessels will be emptied."

"You honor me."

Mother Saint-Raphaël looks away.

Mariette pauses in the hallway to counterpoise a hot teapot, a Japanese cup and saucer, and tightly vased strawflowers on a tray. She then puts an ear to the prioress's door and raps twice. She hears the slight rasp of sandals on the floor.

Sister Aimée juts open the door just an inch and jealously peeks out at the postulant and the red and orange strawflowers. "She's sick," the infirmarian says.

"I have this from Mother Saint-Raphaël. She says Mother Céline should drink some hot tea."

Sister Aimée sighs impatiently and steps outside to get the tray, saying, "I'll be sure to put it by her palliasse."

Mariette pettishly retracts the tray and says, "Mother Saint-Raphaël particularly wanted *me* to give it to the prioress."

"You only?"

"She was thinking it a penance."

Sister Aimée simpers and says, "You see, it is just that Mother Superior is sleeping now."

Mariette smiles insincerely and inches toward the door.

Sister Aimée tries to stop her, hissing, "You are being impossible, Sister!"

"And you are being possessive and invidious!"

"Have it your way," says Sister Aimée. "Again." And she's overwrought with juvenile emotions as she scuttles down the hallway.

Reverend Mother Céline rests on her side on the palliasse as if she could be peering at the tempera painting of Our Mother of Perpetual Help that is hanging on the wall. Wild sleep has tossed aside the gray wool blanket and sheet and twisted her nightgown on her body so that it seems shameless and slatternly. A great gush of blond hair veils her pillow.

Mariette adeptly puts the tray on the sill so there is no more noise than a tap. She sees a sparrow tilt high up in the air and swoop westward out of sight. She then hesitantly turns and stoops over the prioress to assess her illness and pain. She almost feels for the high temperature on Mother Céline's slightly damp forehead, but instead sits on the infirmarian's milking stool. She smells the tang of vomit and urine. And yet she is happy and proud to be there. She thinks, *You see how I love you. Even this way. Especially now.*

She can't take her eyes off the sleeping woman—she who has become for Mariette sight and map and motive. Annie. She sees cracked, parched lips and a trace of sour yellow; a forehead as hot, perhaps, as candle wax; frail eyelids that are redly lettered with tiny capillaries; green veins that tree and knot under the skin of her hands.

The prioress achingly turns on her bed and opens her sorrowing eyes. She keeps them on a high windowpane darkly stippled with hailstones and imperfections. Without looking at Mariette, she asks, "Have you been watching me long?"

"I have brought you hot tea."

She gazes skeptically at the postulant. "Where is Sister Aimée?"

"Elsewhere. Mother Saint-Raphaël sent me. She had me put a medicine in it."

The prioress tries to rise up, but she sinks back to her original position as Mariette pours an orange tea into the Japanese cup. The prioress asks, "Have you read Sext yet?"

"We are having Méridienne now. We can talk."

Mother Céline gets a hint of Alexandria senna aroma and seems upset, but she goes ahead and tastes it. She squints her eyes and sits back. "We haven't talked nearly enough."

"No."

"Your letters . . . have troubled me."

"You weren't supposed to read them."

"I was too curious." She considers Mariette as she would a sudden noise. "You're my sister, but I don't understand you. You aren't understandable." She smiles. "You may be a saint. Saints are like that, I think. Elusive. Other. Upsetting."

"I just am."

"Well, that's good, I guess." She has blood drying on her fingers. She has a water bowl on the floor with a pinked sponge in it. The prioress sips some more tea and pauses for breath, and then she empties the cup and hands it back to the postulant.

Mariette asks, "Are you hungry?"

"I have not eaten for more than a day."

"We had soup."

"I have spewed even that."

"Is it terrible for you now?"

She shrugs. "I have been ill before. I shall be ill again. We are born with it beside us." And then the prioress tightly clutches her stomach with her elbows and forearms. Sudden pain misshapes her face, but Mariette stands there impassively and softly prays as she puts her left hand onto her sister's side.

The prioress shrieks with harrowing pain and slowly rolls away from Mariette's touch. She stays in one position, just catching her breath, and then, as if she has already permitted too much affection and sympathy, she finally says, "You may go."

Mariette gets the tray and goes out, but she smiles back at the prioress as she shuts the door.

December. First Sunday of Advent.

Evening recreation. A squat tallow candle is lit. A yellow thumb of flame trembles on a draft. Reverend Mother Céline is just as sick as she was five days ago, with skin as white as the undersheets, and tiny beads of night sweat that finally break and sketch across her forehead. She hears the sand rasp of sandals on the floor and opens her green eyes.

Mariette is there with a pastry bowl of soap and hot water and an ironed towel. She says nothing as she uncovers the prioress and unties the strings of Annie's nightgown.

The prioress says, "I have become so weak. I hardly belong to myself anymore."

Mariette reaches down to the prioress's knees and inchingly draws the nightgown up over her body, skirting her gaze away from her mother superior's nakedness. She asks, "Was the medicine any help?"

"No."

Mariette sits on the palliasse and puts the bowl of hot water onto her lap. She soaps her own palms. "Shall we send for Papa?"

"God shall be my doctor," the prioress says.

Mariette tenderly washes her sister's hands and arms as a mother would a child's. She pushes a kitchen sponge underwater and then squeezes it dry and softly pets the soap away. She rinses the sponge and soaps it again and then hesitates. "With your permission?"

Mother Céline turns aside a little and Mariette unseeingly washes the prioress's knobbed and ribbed back, her indrawn stomach, her insignificant breasts. The prioress says, "When Jesus washed Saint Peter's feet it was surely a lesson in humility for his apostle, not for himself. We do not like to be done for."

"Especially you, I think."

Annie dresses her breasts with the gray wool blanket and says, "You presume too much."

Mariette just sits there with her palms turned up in her lap. And then she stands up and intricately collects everything she's brought in. She goes out without a word, only pausing at the sill to make a sign of the cross with holy water.

Mass of Saint Nicholas the Great, Bishop, Confessor.

She hears the prioress's sickness through the night.

Mass of the Immaculate Conception of the
Blessed Virgin Mary.

The postulant is sitting with her mother superior in the infirmary, softly reading from the psalms in the company of Sisters Philomène and Hermance. Each is sewing a scroll border on dinner napkins of India cotton. The prioress is sleeping in a freshly laundered and pleated nightgown, her blond hair strewn on the pillow, her hands collected atop a prayerbook and rosary and taut gray wool blanket. Eye-squinting sunshine whitens the room and snows the veils and habits of the novices as Mariette reads: " 'Have mercy upon me, O Lord, for I am weak. My soul is sore vexed, but thou, O Lord, how long? Return, O Lord, deliver my soul. O save me for thy mercy's sake. For in death there is no remembrance of thee, in the grave who shall give thee thanks? I am weary with my groaning; all the night—' "

At that point the infirmary door opens and Dr. Baptiste is there in his English greatcoat with Sister Aimée behind him. His green instrument case is in one hand and his hat in the other and he exudes the flushed red and cold of a hurried horse ride as he looks directly at the sisters and then, with greater interest, at the sick prioress. "She is sleeping?"

Sister Geneviève nods.

Mariette tells her father, "She has a stomach complaint." And when he smirks, she thinks how dull and idiotic she is whenever she's in his presence.

Eyeing the prioress, Dr. Baptiste heaves his instrument case onto a side table. Farm mud crumbles from his high boots and messily scatters across the floor planks as he walks. Although he has dressed in European elegance and bathed himself in perfumes of musk and civet, he carries in his clothes from his morning rounds an odor of illness that is still so offensive that Sister Aimée has cupped a palm over her nose and Sister Philomène inches back her chair half a foot. "She has been vomiting?"

"Yes," Sister Aimée says.

"For how long?"

"Six days," Sister Aimée says, and Dr. Baptiste theatrically turns to her in haughty shock and disdain. And when she does not wither, but intractably stares back at him, Dr. Baptiste shakes his head and holds his ear just above Mother Céline's chapped and parted lips to hear the sighs of her breathing. Tilting his nose down, Dr. Baptiste inhales the prioress's exhalations. "She has been taking guaiacum?"

Sister Aimée glances about interrogatively and says, "We don't know."

"She has." Dr. Baptiste gets up from the prioress and unsnaps the clasp on his case. Underneath the lid is a green velvet drawer holding medicine bottles and jars and silver cups, cannulas, measuring spoons, pestle, and protractor. A second drawer underneath that contains a chrome handsaw, scalpels, scissors, forceps, and a gruesome brace and screw. He gets out an ear trumpet to hear her heart and asks, "Will one of you please find me a wineglass?"

Sister Philomène hurries out.

Dr. Baptiste touches the prioress's wrist in order to estimate a pulse and her eyes flutter open. "*Bonjour*, Annie," he kindly says.

"Who sent for you?" the prioress asks.

"Your predecessor. Mother Saint-Raphaël?"

"*C'est seulement la grippe, Papa.*"

"We shall see. Are you in great pain?"

She gives it thought and agrees.

"You have had this pain for some time?"

"Every now and then."

"With food and without?"

"Either way."

"With your functions: is there blood present?"

Slowly the prioress nods.

Mariette is giving her father the attention she would give a magician. She has imagined him through childhood as the king of a foreign country, but he has changed into a too-heavy man with a glossy mustache and unhealthy white nails and gray cinders of skin blemishes on his winter-reddened face. She sees him fit his unclean palms along Annie's jaw, his squat thumbs tendering the underside of her mouth and then delicately touching back her eyelids so the irises can be examined. "You will stick out your tongue please?"

She complies, and her father scratches the gray coating with his nail, taps her upper teeth and incisors, harshly presses the purple gums. He then daintily unties the strings of her nightgown and slides his right hand underneath to Mother Céline's left armpit. Wretchedly the prioress shuts her eyes as his hand skims down and palms her hurting left breast, slightly lifting and releasing it, nudging his fingers underneath it, and then going over to the other. Squeezing it, the doctor, too, shuts his eyes and says, "Do not be embarrassed."

Sister Philomène then rushes in with a brandy glass. Getting it from her, Dr. Baptiste seems at last to give serious thought to Mariette and the novices. "You ought to go now, all of you. She will want the privacy."

Sister Aimée says uneasily, "One of us must stay. With a man present. Our Rule requires it."

Dr. Baptiste considers Mariette for an overlong moment as though she's a half-forgotten language that he is slow in understanding. "She then," he says.

Sister Aimée sneers in jealousy as she joins Sisters Hermance and Philomène outside and gently shuts the door. Dr. Baptiste hands the brandy glass to his older daughter and asks, "Will you please give me a water specimen?"

She blushes but weakly scooches forward as her father turns away and Mariette rolls the nightgown up to Annie's waist. Annie reaches the brandy glass down between her thighs and Mariette walks to the infirmary's chiffonier in order to get a towel from an upper drawer. She hears a trickle and does not turn. She feels his eyes like hands. Enjoying her. She knows their slow travel and caress.

Annie says, "Papa," and gives him the inch-filled brandy glass as Mariette goes to the prioress with the towel. Dr. Baptiste walks over to one great window and jots some notes in the flooding white sunlight. "Here," Annie whispers, and holds Mariette's hand confidingly against her stomach, and Mariette stares with horror and bewilderment as she perceives the hard tumor just under the skin and sees Annie smile. En-thralled.

Evening and an azure light just above the horizon.

Horse and rider just seen on the road.

Sister Geneviève hunches forward in the choir, a book open on her knees, and Sisters Philomène, Pauline, and Hermance huddle around her, joining in saying "pray for us" as she goes through the Litany of the Blessed Virgin Mary: "Mother most pure, pray for us. Mother most chaste, pray for us. Mother inviolate, pray for us. Mother undefiled, pray for us. Mother most amiable, pray for us. Mother most admirable, pray for us. Mother of good counsel, pray for us—"

Hooves knocking the rough wooden planks of a bridge.

Mariette genuflects upon going into the oratory and gets onto Saint-Pierre's prie-dieu so she can kneel apart from the four novices. She sees Sister Hermance compassionately stare and she tightly shuts her eyes. She prays for an acquittal. She prays for a simple exchange.

Horse gloss and high black boots. Woods and old crack-ling tawny leaves sloshing away from shoed hooves. Trees as snug as fencing and here and there a sketch of an English greatcoat, a starched white shirt cuff, a hand in firm grip on the reins.

Second Sunday of Advent.

Sister Aimée walks onto the red Persian carpet at Prime and tells the sisters that Reverend Mother Céline is still sick, that she's in great pain, that she's lost fifteen pounds or more, that she may, in fact, have cancer. And the whole priory responds as if the infirmarian has blandly announced a murder. Sister Félicité faints. Throughout Mass and Mixt there are handsigns about the illness. Worry harries the sisters in their work and haunts their prayers at Terce and Sext, and at dinner six or more nuns tremulously weep as Sister Monique goes up in the pulpit with *The Rule of Saint Augustine* in order to have them hear again: " 'Let your superior show herself an example to all in good deeds; she is to reprimand those who neglect their work, to give courage to those who are disheartened, to support the weak and to be patient with everyone. She should herself observe the norms of the community and so lead others to respect them too. And let her strive to be loved by you rather than to be feared, although both love and respect are necessary.' "

Mass of Saint Lucy, Virgin, Martyr.

Horsetails of gray smoke rise from the candles at Vespers. The December sun goes down in a blood-red light as it slants upwards through the high, stained windows.

At the half-minute pause following the fifth psalm, Mariette hears soft winds outside, hushing like the skirts of a girl rushing up the stairs. She hears Sister Catherine hissing to herself, *"Jesu. Mon Seigneur Jesu. Cher Jesu."*

And then she flinches and looks down at her hands. She tries to rub the hot sting from one palm with her thumb but the hurt persists like hate inked on a page. Eventually the sisters rise and slowly pass by Mariette as she sits there for a half hour more, hoarding the pain. She hears something skittering along a joist. She hears the red lanterns on the high altar sigh as flames trickily consume them. And then she hears Sister Emmanuelle hesitantly settle beside her and whisper, "Are you praying for our prioress?"

She looks up and simply says, "Yes," and the seamstress pats her approvingly on the wrist.

Third Sunday of Advent.

Mariette twists scissors through heavy black paper in order to snip out a silhouette of Wise Men and a manger that she pastes onto a folded white card. High above the manger, she pastes one of Sister Hermance's gold stars, and then she writes inside, *"Joyeux Noël, Papa!"* She pauses and thinks, but no further phrases come, and so she puts the card as it is inside an envelope.

Mass of Saint Lazarus, Disciple.

Twenty minutes into Mixt, Mother Saint-Raphaël opens the great door to the dining hall and grins as she announces, "She has gotten better."

And Mother Céline is abruptly there in her habit and veil, the skull beneath her skin plainly visible, getting support from Sister Aimée as she walks falteringly to her place. Sisters rise up to kiss her cheek and hands or just to cheer and applaud her, and the prioress briefly smiles. She seems twice her age as she greets the sisters with a half wave and then hesitantly sits.

Sister Saint-Léon's gray eyes shine with tears of joy as she kneels next to Mother Céline and asks, "Oh, are you truly improved?"

"Yes," she says. "Christ be praised."

Ember Day. Mass of Saint Liberatus, Martyr.

In her dream Mariette is pregnant and her great breasts ache with milk, but she holds the infant Christ to them and he smiles as he feeds on her. And then she hears a dish crash to the floor and she thinks he was in a toddler's chair and she was a girl in a housedress but she doesn't know why the dish crashed and she worries and she wakes. She listens, but all is silence.

Twenty minutes before the second rising, Sister Philomène gets up from her kneeler in the oratory and goes down the hallway toward the house of the externs to wake up Sister Claudine. She softly passes the prioress's suite before she notices the door ajar and that she can just see a hand on the floor. She pushes inside and finds Mother Céline fallen there. The prioress tiredly smiles up at the novice and says, "Please, help me."

Mariette is still in her nightgown and her chocolate-brown hair is wild as she gets a black habit from her great pine armoire. Her cell is so cold with December that she can see her breath in the air. She hears two taps on her door and opens it.

Sister Philomène is standing there. She gives the hand-signs, *Come, prioress.* And Mariette sees that Sister Philomène's hands are red with blood.

Everyone in the priory is permitted five minutes with Mother Céline in the heated infirmary, but some of the professed nuns have tarried for half an hour or more, so Mariette is forced to go in with Sisters Hermance, Geneviève, Léocadie, and Pauline when the last visitation is held just before Compline. She finds the prioress sitting up in a gray habit and black shawl, in an Adirondack chair hauled in from the yard. Commercial papers are shuffled up under her folded hands, and on a side table are Dr. Baptiste's prescriptions of Hostetter's Stomach Bitters and Mrs. Winslow's Soothing Syrup, a flavored medicine for teething babies that he knows is basically morphine. In accordance with the rules and customs of the order, a plain wood coffin has been hastily carpentered by Sister Marie-Madeleine and then put on sawhorses in the room to inspire contemplation and a Christian acceptance of death. Mother Céline sleepily rambles so she won't have to hear Sister Geneviève's praise or witness Sisters Hermance and Pauline weeping freely at her feet.

Mariette jealously looks at the novices as Annie tells them that Sister Antoinette reports she'll be shipping communion wines to upstate parishes by April. She tells them the priory is a major beneficiary of a Catholic woman's estate. She says she hopes Mother Saint-Raphaël will agree to be their prioress again, she is so good at paperwork. She says she's impatient for God to take her, she thinks it's like having all the glorious smells of a Christmas feast but having the tastes withheld. And then the chimes ring for Compline and the prioress holds up her hand for the blessing, "*Adjutorium nostrum in nomine Domini.*"

And Mariette shuts her eyes as she hears the chorus, "*Qui fecit coelum et terram.*"

Mass of Saint Ischyrion, Martyr.

Fourth Sunday of Advent.

Exhausted, Mother Céline pushes away a dish of half-eaten food on her tray and tilts back against four pillows on her palliasse as she faintly smiles at Mariette. She says, "I have a memory of you when you were five and I was just making my profession. You and Papa visited me here and he was called away, I think, and you and I tried to pass the hour in a children's game you made up. You told me I was a princess and had been put inside a jail that was just four walls and a locked door. And I was to try and get out. 'I'll scream for help,' I said, 'and a handsome prince will save me.' And you said, 'There's no one around to hear you.' 'Well then,' I said, 'I'll kick at the door until it breaks.' But you said, 'The door's made of iron and you can pound and pound but it won't be hurt.' 'I'll look on the floor and find a key,' I said, and you said I could indeed do that, but the key wouldn't fit the lock. And I said, 'You're making this so *difficult*, Mariette.' You asked if I really and truly wanted to get out, and I told you that I did. And then you said, 'The jail has no ceiling. And you have wings. And you fly.' "

Christmas Eve.

Stillness. And then first rising.

Mariette is naked. Moonlight glints along a short passage of tangled wire that is as intricate as a signature, that is taut enough to ingrain itself in the skin underneath her breasts. One upper thigh is blackly streaked with blood that is seeping from the rabbit wire that is tied just below her sex.

She sits on the palliasse and loosens the persecutions. She uses a handkerchief to paint away the blood and the pink tracks along her skin. She stows the wires beneath her straw palliasse and gets into her habit.

She goes out in the hallway as Sisters Marthe and Saint-Estèphe are heading toward the washroom. She puzzles over something she sees and hurries her steps.

Sister Pauline holds her hands to her face, and farther down the hallway, Sisters Honoré and Saint-Stanislas are standing at the infirmary door, dully staring inside the room as Père Marriott sidesteps by them in a cassock and purple stole.

Mariette hesitates.

The sisters part so she can pass into the room, but Mariette halts and turns and scurries back to her cell.

Sister Agnès, Sister Anne, and Sister Emmanuelle silently work on Mother Céline. Hands pursue other hands in slipping the nightgown up over her yawing head, sleeking her skin and hair with vinegar and perfume of bergamot, dressing her in a clean gray habit and black veil and winter cape. She is raised up and carried aside one step and nestled into the pinewood coffin. Sister Agnès pretties some skewed pleats and folds and then the sisters bow deeply and walk out with their hands in prayer at their chins.

Late morning.

Six tall candles flank the pinewood coffin as the former prioress lies feet-first before the high altar and just inside the oratory. Hothouse flowers from Ithaca have been tucked inside her folded arms.

Sisters Catherine and Zélie are hurriedly cloaking the church in black cretonne.

Six village women are slumped here and there in pews, whispering their rosaries for the Annette Baptiste they knew and the prioress they saw on great feasts.

Workmen have chopped a hole in the hard earth with picks and spades and now stand in the church's apse with their hats in their hands.

Dr. Baptiste goes up to the oaken grille and hangs on it with all his fingers for a half hour or more.

It has pleased God to call to Himself our dear

REVEREND MOTHER CÉLINE

who died in the service of the Blessed Virgin Mary

on December 24, 1906,

in the priory of Our Lady of Sorrows

in the 37th year of her age

and the 15th of her religious profession.

At the hour of Christ's death on the cross, the oak doors of the oratory are opened and the great bell tolls as the Sisters of the Crucifixion proceed inside, their faces hidden behind sheer black veils.

Wearing a hooded black cope over his vestments, Père Marriott haltingly walks from the sacristy with a book in his hands, genuflects to Christ in the tabernacle, and blesses the whole priory of sisters behind the grille. He then reads: " 'Come to our sister's assistance, you saints of God. Come forth to meet her, you angels of the Lord; receive her soul and offer it in the sight of the most High.' "

Mother Saint-Raphaël stands at the head of the coffin and settles her hands upon it. "May Christ who has called you, Sister Céline, now receive His handmaid, and may all the angels lead you to Abraham's bosom."

The Sisters of the Crucifixion respond, "Receive her soul and offer it in the sight of the Most High."

Mother Saint-Raphaël retreats from the coffin as the six externs approach it in half-steps. "Eternal rest grant to our sister, O Lord."

"And let perpetual light shine upon her."

After the Requiem Mass and just before sundown, the former prioress is taken past the old printery and the green ice of the marsh to the Order's cemetery. Hard sleet hisses against the trees. The eastern skies are as black as charred wood.

Dr. Baptiste and a handful of villagers trudge up a hillside behind the sisters and kneel with them as Père Marriott completes the interment prayers and blesses the pinewood coffin with holy water. Half the priory is openly weeping and half are staring wonderingly at Mariette as she kneels and prays as if in a trance.

Mother Saint-Raphaël hands Sister Aimée the book of rituals and the infirmarian tonelessly reads, " 'Grant, O Lord, we beseech You, that while we lament the departure from this life of our sister, we may recall that we shall all follow her one day. Give us grace to prepare for that final hour with a devout and holy life, and teach us to watch and pray that when Your summons comes we may go forth to meet our bridegroom and enter with Him into life everlasting."

And then, as four workmen spade hardened earth onto the box, Mother Saint-Raphaël heads a solemn procession back to the oratory for Vespers and the chant of the psalms.

And there is Christmas Mass at midnight. And going to the haustus room for ginger cookies and sham champagne, and giving Sister Philomène an English lip salve Mariette has made from sweet oil and the attar of roses. And Mother Saint-Raphaël gives Mariette a sympathy card with an inscription from the Beatitudes: "Blessed are they that mourn: for they shall be comforted." And then all go to their cells.

Henri Marriott seeks a kind of sustenance in prayer and kneels for an hour on the hard cold penance of the sacristy floor. And when he gets up, he peers through the grille and sees Mariette in the night of the oratory, intently staring at the crucifix above the high altar, her hands spread wide as if she were nailed just as Christ was. He puts on his biretta and overcoat and half genuflects with difficulty and goes back to the priest's house.

Blood scribbles down her wrists and ankles and scrawls like red handwriting on the floor.

Part 3

Moonlessness. Starlessness.

Matins and Lauds of Our Lady's Office. And then silence.

Harried snow. Creaking trees.

Chill winds flute through the chimney flues. Kitchen smoke flails in the air.

Empty fields shine like white satin sheets.

Hard gusts zing against an iron shovel.

The blood-red leaf of a poison sumac is freed and scutters up against the shiplap on the old printery.

Second rising.

Windowpanes yelp with hard polish and four or five sisters peer outside.

Sister Pauline hovers over a flittering matchstick as she hustles down the darkened hallway, feeding the blue and yellow flame to the hallway's high, jarred candles.

*　　　*　　　*

Sisters Ange and Sabine and Saint-Stanislas huddle between horses in the stall, heating their hands on the horse flanks.

Sister Geneviève pours hot water into a great tin washing bowl and Sister Monique holds her face inside a pale blossom of steam.

Henri Marriott is hunched at the kitchen table in the priest's house, in round spectacles that shine like half-dollars, hunting letters on his great black typewriter's keyboard. Each word clacks as loudly as handled dishware but underneath he hears the house door creak wide. "Hello?" he calls, and with difficulty turns around in his chair.

Mariette is there, just inside the door, holding a hand in a hand like a pink teacup and saucer. She falteringly walks toward him and he sees she has no sandals on.

Each foot is torn with injury. Each leaves a red print of blood on the floor.

—I have no memories of that.

—Were you in ecstasy?

—Is it for me to say?

—Please tell us what you remember.

—Midnight Mass. And praying, in the oratory.

—And after that?

—Just being in the infirmary.

—While you were being examined.

—Yes; then.

—When you came to me, have you heard what you said?

She holds out her blood-painted hands like a present and she smiles crazily as she says, "Oh, look at what Jesus has done to me!"

*　　　*　　　*

Reverend Mother Saint-Raphaël hammers her walking cane on the floor planks as she hurries down the hallway ahead of Père Marriott who is still in his soot-black wool coat and biretta, an extreme unction kit in his hand.

Four novices and three sisters are jammed at the infirmary door, whispering hearsay as they peek inside. Sister Hermance turns and hints with a cough and the sisters at the doorway shamefully part for the new prioress. She worriedly pauses until their priest has caught up and then she precedes him inside the room, patting her fingertips onto the holy water sponge and making the sign of the cross.

Sister Saint-Denis is high up on a sill, hanging gray privacy blankets over the tall and brilliant windows. With Mariette is Sister Aimée. She has taken off the postulant's black headscarf and habit and underthings and is folding them carefully inside white butcher's paper and tying it up with yarn.

The postulant herself is in a white bathrobe and sitting up against four pillows because she gasps for breath if she is flat on her back. Eyes shining with tenderness, hoarsely and hushfully speaking half-sentences, Mariette stares up into nothingness like a teenaged girl newly intrigued with herself, or as if she has finally heard her heart and is being haunted by it. Windings of torn cloth hide palms that are weakly turned up in her lap, a gray blanket tents her feet, and a hand towel is twisted over her brow. Sister Saint-Denis has undone Mariette's dark brown hair so that it is troublingly disordered against the white pillowcase, but her skin is as radiant and pink with health as if she'd just strolled in from a skate.

Mother Saint-Raphaël asks, "Is she in pain?"

"Especially in her hands," Sister Aimée says. "The holes are hideous."

"And her side, too?"

"Everything," Sister Aimée says.

"Is it possible she's done this to herself?"

Sister Aimée simply folds a hand towel beside a pillow and pretends she hasn't heard.

Speaking as she would to a child, the prioress harshly asks the postulant, "Listen to me, Mariette. Is this a true experience? Have you helped it in any way?"

Mariette says nothing.

"She's in a trance," Sister Aimée says.

Père Marriott takes a six-foot purple stole from his extreme unction kit and kisses it while softly reciting the Latin prayer that one day God will be pleased to clothe him in the blessed immortality forfeited by humanity's first parents. Yoking his neck with the stole, he turns and hesitates with embarrassment before saying to the prioress, "We will have to look at her wounds."

Mother Saint-Raphaël swings toward Sister Saint-Denis as she is getting down from the sill, and she urges her to please bring the stool over for their priest and then go. Sister Saint-Denis humbly obeys but beams at Mariette from the hallway as she shuts the door.

Hunching down on the stool next to the postulant, Père Marriott tilts his ear to hear her whispering sentences he cannot understand. And then he dourly nods to Sister Aimée, who unties the white bathrobe and undoors the left half and turns up a hand towel that is just below Mariette's full left breast.

She is bleeding enough that Sister Aimée has to touch the wound again with the hand towel for the priest to see a hand-width laceration between the fifth and sixth ribs.

"Is it deep?" the priest asks.

"Christ's was deeper," Sister Aimée says.

"We shall not draw comparisons, please," Mother Saint-Raphaël corrects. She is standing behind them, her hands in her sleeves, and honoring their rule for custody of the eyes by holding her stare on the floor.

Père Marriott asks, "Sister Aimée. Would you be kind enough to describe the injuries?"

She states, "We see she has a jagged wound just above the fifth costal cartilage. I haven't measured it but I'd estimate it to be four inches long and a quarter-inch deep, just past the subcutaneous tissue, but she imagines she feels it interfering whenever she inhales. She's bleeding, but not inordinately, hardly three ounces so far. We see some peculiarities here, too. We'd expect to see reddening, erosion, or an inflammatory reaction in the zone of skin around the tear. We don't."

"And why is that?"

"I have no idea."

The priest returns the hand towel and hides Mariette's nakedness. And then, having for the first time felt her heat, he looks up at Sister Aimée with horror and surprise and again puts his hand to the white bathrobe and then to the postulant's neck. "She's so hot!"

"She has a temperature. We'd expect that."

"Have you taken her pulse, Sister?"

"Erratic. We counted one hundred eighty beats per minute at one time, a hundred and ten the next, and then as slow as sixty. Even dreaming could do that, though."

"She's in no danger then?"

"She's excited, that's all." She draws away the gray blanket and gingerly begins unbandaging the postulant's feet and hands.

—You were aware of us then.

—I heard Sister Aimée. And it hurt when you touched his wounds.

—His.

—Embodied by me, but not mine.

*   *   *

Each is slightly greater than the size of a penny or just about the injury a timber spike would make if hammered hard and cleanly into human flesh. Each is approximately in the same place, just inside the first bone of the hand and angling down through the furrow in the palm to a slight gap where the first finger joins the wrist. Each foot wound is between the first and second metatarsal and through the high dorsal ridge to the instep, as if Mariette's knees had been brought up and her soles held flush to a flat surface before spikes had been pounded through each foot.

Weeping from the holes is a pinkish serum and blood that the priest channels into a phial until he has half an inch. He puts it into his cassock pocket, then firmly presses the skin around Mariette's hand wounds while peering up at the postulant to see if she'll wince at the pain. She gives no sign that he's even there.

"She's bleeding so little, really," Père Marriott says. "Don't you find that odd?"

"I have no training for this," Sister Aimée says. And when she sees him still looking at her, she tries, "In India, I hear, there are some people who can stop their bleeding just by thinking about it." She opens a wooden case of medicines and asks, "Shall I dress her wounds?"

Wiping his reddened fingertips with his handkerchief, the old priest thinks about their options and says experimentally, "Yes, do."

But when Sister Aimée squeezes a zinc ointment onto the postulant's hand, she hears Mariette scream with such horror and pain that she withholds the medicine and looks for further information from their priest. "Shall we let her be?" she asks.

"We seem to have no choice," he says, and withdraws his head from under his stole.

Mother Saint-Raphaël is facing an instrument tray and faintly ticking the chrome-bright points of the forceps and scissors there as she thinks. And when she turns to instruct the infirmarian she is again fierce and formidable, saying Sister Aimée is to stay with the postulant until they pray Nones; she'll assign other sisters to be with Mariette from then on. When Mariette is herself again, she may join the sisters in their refectory and choir, but she shall be accompanied wherever else she goes. And no one is to speak or write of this to those outside the priory. She tells Sister Aimée, "We do this, we keep watch, for Mariette's own protection. She is weak now. She is in distress. And she has hurt herself; just that."

Sister Agnès talks about Mariette to Sister Ange across the high-railed fence of the horse paddock. She hears the Angelus bell begin ringing but the extern just keeps talking over the campanile's noise.

Sister Saint-Denis, Honoré, Saint-Estèphe, and Monique have been in high temper about the postulant while polishing the chapter room's dark wooden pieces with flaxseed oil and red flannel. Hearing the Angelus bell too late, Sister Saint-Denis hurriedly crosses herself, and there is a flint of hurt in her eye as she offers, "The angel of the Lord declared unto Mary."

The sisters respond in dull chorus, "And she conceived of the Holy Ghost."

Père Marriott stands darkly alone on the herringboned brick sidewalk just outside his house with four library books in his hands, praying an Ave Maria and inhaling the heaven smell of fresh snow as he says, "Behold the handmaid of the Lord."

Sister Aimée holds a sponge and a chrome bowl in her hands as she looks at the yard through a chink between the gray blankets. White pillows of snow are there where rough stones used to be. She sees juncos feeding on tossed green peas. And she turns with shock when she hears Mariette say in a trance, "Be it done unto me according to thy word."

Mother Saint-Raphaël is rapidly writing at her great pecan desk with a green fountain pen, hearing the Angelus being said by two externs in the hall. She halts her pen to pray an Ave Maria and then hides her face in her hands. She hears Sister Zélie say, "And the Word was made flesh." And she hears Sister Claudine say, "And dwelt amongst us." And then she prays another Ave Maria and returns to her letter.

Our Lady of Sorrows Convent
Arcadia, New York

Dec. 25th, 1906

Mother Christine
Superior, The Sisters of the Crucifixion
Villa Rossignol
Louvain, Belgium

Most Reverend Mother General:

The blessings and grace of Our Lord Jesus Christ be always to our favor and assistance.

I have news of such gravity that I have been almost too grief-stricken to begin. And yet it has befallen me to inform you that our dear Reverend Mother Céline died some time after Lauds on Monday, December 24th, following a brief illness. She had prayed and worked tirelessly under our Holy Rule for fifteen years and she was for an illustrious period our cherished Mother Superior here. We shall miss her so much.

Elected at Chapter to be our new prioress was the

present writer, a terrible sinner and the Queen of Heaven's most worthless servant, whom Our Lord has burdened before with leadership (1891–1902). I rejoice, however, in doing again what I have done my best to do in the past, believing that all is possible with Christ and hoping that I shall always know His holy will.

I have other troubling news as well. We have in our priory here a seventeen-year-old postulant named Mariette Baptiste—sister in blood to our late prioress—who is said to have been given the holy wounds of Christ's passion on the Cross! I have heard that she's written fantastic letters that told of her having experienced interior conversations and trances since she asked to be admitted into the Sisters of the Crucifixion, and there are some professed nuns and novices to whom she has given an impression of great saintliness before she was granted the purported stigmata.

I shall refrain from comment on the faithfulness and credibility of their testimonies on Mariette's behalf, nor need I mention the postulant's flair for the dramatic and her turbulent psychological state at the time of her dear sister's illness and premature death. She was under my purview when I was Mistress of Novices so she has not been without scrutiny or merited correction, but I cannot talk freely about her piety and orthodoxy without jeopardizing the precious bonds of intimacy that have been established between the pliant and unformed soul and her formation director. With open mind, however, I shall interview the postulant and our sisters in the priory in order to determine whether Mariette is truly as she seems and whether she possesses the authentic spiritual foundation and exemplary rectitude that God's grace presupposes.

What must be reported has been reported. Please do convey our solicitudes to Sister Irène and Sister Barbe who are studying theology with you there in our beloved Mother-

house. Please tell all who hold us dear that we are thriving
here with abundant prayer and blessings and the practice
of heroic virtues. May Our Lady guide our hearts and
minds in these trying times.

Yours humbly on behalf of God our Father, to Whom
alone be glory and honor forever. Amen.

Sr. Saint-Raphaël
Mother Superior

Tallow candles.

Skin like the moon.

Eye sockets tinged with green. Eyelids lightly fluttering in dream.

The postulant's mouth is sore and cracked and welted purple by her own teeth.

Sighs and caws to her slow and intricate breathing.

Sister Hermance is hooking and knotting lace as she primly sits on a stool in night watch. She collapses her handiwork in her lap and just stares with poignance at Mariette. She's about to get up but pauses. She gives it some thought and gets up after all, setting her lace aside and then holding on to Mariette's left hand like a tender nurse reading a pulse. She tilts her head to fondly inspect Mariette, petting her brow and touching a dark hair away from her cheek. She hesitates for a second and then she unwraps the torn strips of cloth from a hand that is stained as red as a dyer's.

A great copper verrière is on the floor. Sister Hermance retrieves a ball sponge from the verrière and wrings it tight before softly daubing at the hand wound. She peers at it and at Mariette. She whispers, "I just have to see." And then she gently lowers Mariette's left hand until it is submerged in pink water.

Blood seeps silkily from the hand wound, turning and rumpling underwater until it gradually untangles into nothing more than color.

"I hope you're not angry," she says. "We all were wondering. We didn't think it would be so real."

She lifts up the postulant's hand and presses it into her habit as she considers Mariette. "We aren't amazed. We thought you were different from the first."

She pets Mariette's wrist and kisses a knuckle. She whispers, "We are so privileged." She holds the palm open and kisses it. "You have turned your face from me too often. You have been frightened by my affection."

With reverence Sister Hermance licks the blood inside the hand wound. "I have tasted you. See?" Tears streak shining paths down her cheeks as she says, "Ever since I first met you, I have loved you more than myself."

Half a minute later she says, "You know this is true."

She stares at Mariette's sleep and whispers, "You have been a sacrament to me."

Mass of Saint Stephen, the First Martyr.

An hour before sunrise Sister Anne knocks on the priest's door and he hurriedly opens it, hoisting up a kerosene lamp. "Enter, Sister."

She hesitates and does.

"Smell," he says. "The air."

She skeptically complies. Tobacco smoke and kerosene and maleness, but over it a pretty and otherly scent. With great surprise she asks, "Is it *perfume?*"

"Yes. What kind?"

She permits herself another step inside and pauses. "Easter lilies?"

Père Marriott smiles and says, "Walk about now, Sister. Find the perfume for me."

Sister Anne tilts her head and trains her nose on his four-poster bed. She walks up to it and pauses and then lifts up the lid on a floor trunk that hides his dirty things. She squats and interestedly roots among his underwear and boot socks and soutane and then holds a pressed handkerchief up to her nose. She looks up to see Père Marriott smiling.

"Yes," he says. "Exactly."

Sister Anne stares at the handkerchief and sees it has been blotted here and there with blood.

While the sisters line up outside the oratory for Prime, the prioress greets them with handsigns and touches and smiles. And then she anxiously looks past the sisters to the hallway.

Mariette is tottering toward them, her hands half-mittened in knitted wool, hiding the hurt in her dressed and sandalless feet by hitting down on only the heels and sides. She seems flushed and surprisingly healthy, but ashamed of the hushed attention of the sisters, and she shies from their fawning and tearful stares as she achieves her place in front of the choir and the great brass bell in the campanile rings.

At Mixt she neither drinks nor eats. Each of the sisters furtively stares at her as she tranquilly sits in post-Communion meditation with her hands immersed in her habit. *Lectio* has been halted for the morning, so there is only the Great Silence and the tinks of cutlery, but handsigns are being traded as the sisters lard their hunks of bread or fold and ring their dinner napkins. When the prioress stands, all rise up with her for the blessing, and then Sister Aimée gives Mariette the handsigns, *You, infirmary.*

Mariette sits impassively at a white-enameled table and stares at a blush-red sun just coming up through trees as thin as hatpins. Sister Aimée sits opposite and holds her hand like a fortune-teller as she takes off the half-mitten and hesitantly touches the hardening scab where only hours ago the nail hole was. She is astonished and then she is silent. Within a tin bowl beside her are soft cotton balls soaking up peroxide. She gets one and squeezes it and roughly abrades the dried blood from Mariette's palm until she's sure she's seen the healing of weeks in just one day. She tries to read Mariette's face, and then she says, "I'll have to see your foot."

"Which?"

The infirmarian looks for a trick and tries, "Your left."

Mariette unties the dressings and Sister Aimée kneels to find the healing there, too. She pauses and asks, "What are you up to?"

"Up to?"

Sister Aimée's sleepless eyelids open and shut like dull scissors. "You were supposed to stay put but you sneaked out this morning. Why?"

"Simply for Mass and Holy Communion."

Sister Aimée stares at her with honest interest and then she stands. "You truly amaze me."

"I have work to do," Mariette says.

She tries to smile at the postulant as she asks, "Then why are you still here?"

Mariette is sent after Terce to the haustus room, where she helps Sisters Agnès and Emmanuelle waterproof the sisters' cloaks with paintbrushes and a tin pail of hot linseed oil and litharge. Whenever Mariette looks up, she sees Sister Emmanuelle simpering at her, and there are times when Mariette flattens cloth on the floor or shakes a paintbrush inside the tin pail that Sister Emmanuelle pretends inadvertence in order to touch her honored hands. Sister Agnès, though, is prattling on as if nothing at all has changed, telling them that good housekeepers put one day between washing and ironing if they want to prolong their lives, that half a cup of vinegar in the kettle water will make an old goose cook up just as quick as a gosling, and that blood will be subtracted from fabrics if you rub in some pepsin first and then steep them in lukewarm water.

Sister Emmanuelle upbraids the laundress by saying, "You are being uncouth, Sister Agnès."

"*Am* I? How?"

"Talking of bloodstains! Here! Now!"

"Please don't," says Mariette. And just then Sister Félicité is at the haustus room's door, reporting that the postulant is expected at the priest's house.

"Ho, get used to it, dearie," Sister Agnès says. "You're going to be the topic here. We'll be sniffing after you like hounds."

In the priest's house, four books are on the kitchen table, a dish towel hides his typewriter, the teakettle warbles and trills on the iron stove until Père Marriott hoists it off. "We are having English tea," he says. "You'll have to take milk with it; that's the English part." Looking over his shoulder, he says, "You may sit."

She does. She inhales and her faintness passes. She touches the books and tilts her head to read their spines. Each is in French: *Annales de médicine universelle, Autobiographie d'une hystérique possédée,* book two of *Esprit des saintes illustres,* and one volume of *La stigmatisation, l'etase divine, les miracles de Lourdes, response aux libres penseurs.*

The priest slides a tarnished spoon and frail teacup and saucer toward Mariette before sighing and falling into a hard wooden chair. With horror he says, "I have forgotten the sugar!"

"Oh, don't get it for me."

"Sister Dominique has favored us with a bowl of *kiss* pudding. Have you heard of that, kiss pudding?"

"Coconut sprinkled on top?"

"Exactly! Like snowflakes."

She smiles and sips just a bit of her orange pekoe tea.

"Well," the priest says. "Isn't this pleasant?"

"Yes."

He clinks his spoon around his teacup and then stains his folded napkin tan with it. She can see a freakish reflection of him in the shine of his spoon's silver bowl. Wood in the stove is whistling. Père Marriott finally says, "Your health is fine?"

She smiles. "Except for the holes in my hands and feet."

He blushes and then shades into humorlessness, broodingly turning his teacup with his thumbs. "I have some more questions I'll have to ask you."

Mariette says nothing. She holds the hurt in her hands like a kitten.

"Surely you were expecting that."

"Everything has been a great surprise to me."

"Yes," he says, and grins uneasily, showing gray teeth that are slightly twisted and crossed. "Well, let me begin there, Mariette. You see, I hunted these books in the scriptorium and when I took them out I heard from Sister Marguerite that she's seen you reading these same four books. She quite frankly finds that perplexing. I have an explanation but I would prefer, of course, to hear yours."

"I have had forebodings about it."

"You have had premonitions?"

"I heard his voice."

Père Marriott stares at her for a moment and moves on. "Well, yes. Was there anything, uh, physical?"

"Itching and burning in my hands and feet."

"And then quite suddenly the bleeding?"

"Yes." She thinks of her father bluntly talking of human biology as the dinner plates were cleared. She remembers how his hard white shirt cuffs would often be brownly spotted with some patient's blood.

"You aren't taking your tea, Mariette."

"I haven't been drinking much lately."

"Are you hungry? Would you like some kiss pudding?"

"Everything's fine."

"Excellent," he says, and scratches whiskers under his jaw as he thinks. "Wasn't it surprising that this happened at Christmas?"

"No."

"Explain, please."

"We celebrate the Word being made incarnate then."

"But it is such a joyful day!"

"We give gifts to our family and friends. And these are God's gifts to me."

He hooks his spectacles over his ears and hunts his book stack until he finds one that he handles like a connoisseur, admiring its green leather binding and the gossamer feel of its pages. At last he tilts his nose down and stares over his brass wire rims to ask, "Are you acquainted enough with the books you and I have read, Mariette, to say you have acquired the wounds that have been called the stigmata?"

"Agreeing would make me seem grandiose."

"Even so, you must be quite proud to be in the company of Saint Francis of Assisi, Saint Catherine of Siena, Saint Rita, so many other holy people."

"Everything is his doing. I have nothing to do with it."

"And yet I still wonder how you feel about it."

She looks just to the right of him in seeking an answer. She holds her stare on a dulled housefly blundering at a frosted window, but she is all inwardness and certainty. "Worried," she says. "Humbled. Embarrassed. I truly don't understand it."

The priest smiles. "We don't have to understand what God is doing for God to be able to do it." Père Marriott deliberately resettles his teacup in the saucer. "You have been given those things which theologians call *gratiae gratis datae,* or favors freely bestowed by God. We do not earn or warrant them. The Church cannot say that you are *saintly* because of these injuries any more than she would hazard to say that Sister Saint-Pierre, for example, is unholy because she is without them. In history, you see, these wounds have been found in some very unworthy people. And it is often hard to tell whether these things are not just illusions brought on by abnormal sensibilities and neurosis. You see how it follows? Hmm? Have I made myself understood?"

"Yes."

"I have so many questions, though."

"Me too."

"We know, for example, that Christ's crucifixion happened in just one way, and yet history tells us that the five wounds appear differently both in size and location in the hundreds of people who have been given them. You have not been given the crown of thorns, for example, nor the forty lashes. And why is that? Is the human personality one component of the mystery? We don't know. And why are there so many women and so few men? And how is it that the great contemplative orders, the Carthusians, the Trappists, the Benedictines, have practically no examples of the phenomena? The Church and medicine are both silent."

Sister Anne knocks twice at the door while opening it to slap the priest's mail onto a Shaker table. She gives Mariette a fraught look and says, "Oh, forgive me," and the old priest gazes without forgiveness until she finally goes.

"And so," he says. "I have another question. You are praying hard, so hard, and you are hearing God inside your head perhaps. We'll say you are in ecstasy. Will you please tell how it is for you at that point?"

Evasively she travels her fingers over four or five water

rings that have stained the oaken table. She then stands with her feet flat on the floor and walks without hurt or hindrance to a half-curtained window framing soft white pastures and flesh-pale skies and pinkish trees without hunters in them.

"In prayer I float out of myself. I seek God with a great yearning, like an orphan child pursuing her true mother. I have lost my body; I don't know where I am or even if I am now human or spirit. A sweet power is drawing me, a great and beautiful force that is effortless but insistent. I flush with excitement and a balm of tenderness seems to flow over me. And when I have gotten to a fullness of joy and peace and tranquillity, then I know I have been possessed by Jesus and have completely lost myself in him. Oh, what a blissful abandonment it is! Everything in my being tells me to stay there. Every thought I have is of his infinite perfection. Every feeling I have is of his kindness and heavenly love. Every dream I have had is realized in him. Hours may pass, but I have no sense of tiredness or pain or needs of any kind. Exquisite contentment enthralls me. I have no use for speech except to praise him. I have no desires except to be held there by him forever. I have a vision of him but I cannot see his face or his form, only an infinite light and goodness. I hear his voice in an interior way, his words have sweetness and charm but no sound, and yet they are more felt and permanent in my soul than if I heard Jesus pronounce them. And there are harder times during prayer when I behold my life as if it were a book of hundreds of pages that faithfully recall all my faults and failings. And then such a great sorrow for my sins takes possession of me that it seems to me I would rather die a horrible death than ever sin against God again."

She hesitates and, blushing with embarrassment, turns to the priest as if she's just remembered that he's there. Père Marriott is quiet for a moment and heaves himself up. "Shall I get you more tea?"

She shakes her head.

"Each phrase there, was it your own?"

"Excuse me?"

He does not turn, but tips the teakettle so discreetly that the hot water twines soundlessly into his cup. "Isn't it possible for me to believe you had formulated that answer in your head before visiting me here? You could have *borrowed*, for example, from the books you have been reading."

"Yes, it *is* possible for you to believe that."

"And is there another explanation?"

"Christ was my teacher."

Expressionlessly, he carries his teacup back to the kitchen table while saying, "Tell me how it was, praying, just yesterday."

She hears firewood wheezing and thudding apart inside the iron stove. She sees red peppers on his kitchen sill and a knife and fork upright inside a milky glass. "I felt greatly upset at first because of Annie, Mother Céline; but as I began to meditate on the crucifixion and Christ's own trials in this world, I became rapt in thought and I found myself again before Jesus, who was suffering such terrible pain. He was horrible with blood and his breathing was hard and troubled, but his pain had less to do with that than with his human sense of failure, injustice, and loneliness. An unquenchable desire to join him in his agonies took hold of me then, as if I could halve his afflictions by sharing them, and I beseeched Jesus to grant me that grace. And, in his great kindness, he gratified me at once. Kneeling there below his cross, I saw that blood no longer issued from his wounds, but only flashing light as hot as fire. And all of a sudden I felt a keen hurt as those flames touched my hands and feet and heart. I have never felt such pain before, and I have never been so happy. I have no memories of the hours passing, I have only the memories of a kind of pleasure and contentment I haven't ever known, a kind that made me love the world as he does, and hearing him whisper just before dawn that I ought to go to you."

"Christ mentioned my name?"

" 'See Père Marriott,' he said."

"Well, that makes me very happy," the old priest says, and then he half rotates in his chair and takes off his round spectacles.

She hears Sister Anne ringing the tocsin for Sext but before she asks permission to go, she says, "When the pains started in September, I had no idea what they truly meant. And then I persuaded myself that all sisters espoused to Christ by their vows would have experienced his wounds. You can't know how stupid and innocent I was! Even yesterday, even after all my reading, I had no true understanding of what was happening to me and at first I hoped to keep it secret, but Christ told me that was impossible in the midst of the priory and with my hands and feet bleeding freely. And now I wonder if I haven't made it all up in some way, or if it's even possible."

Père Marriott slowly puts on his glasses and thinks for half a minute and then smiles up at her as he says, "I don't believe it's possible. I do believe it happened."

Mass of the Holy Innocents, Martyrs.

Four or five minutes into collation, Sister Saint-Estèphe finishes the reading of *The Soul's Journey into God* by Saint Bonaventure, shuts the book, and hobbles down to the dining room floor. Mariette, whose turn it is next, then stands and curtsies to the prioress and tries not to show the pain in her feet as she hushes across to the great tree of the pulpit and goes up.

She hears a kitchen door, Sister Saint-Luc humming her

handsigns, hot coffee purling into a lifted tin cup, and just below the pulpit a scritching knife. She breathes in and recites:

"We begin tonight *The Book of Privy Counseling* by an
unknown Christian mystic from the fourteenth century.

"Chapter one. 'When you go apart to be alone for prayer,
put from your mind everything you have been doing or plan to
do. Reject all thoughts, be they good or be they evil. Do not
pray with words unless you are really drawn to this; or if you
do pray with words, pay no attention to whether they are many
or few. Do not weigh them or their meaning. Do not be con-
cerned about what kind of prayers you use, for it is unimpor-
tant whether or not they are official liturgical prayers, psalms,
hymns, or anthems; whether they are for particular or general
intentions; or whether you formulate them interiorly, by
thoughts, or express them aloud, in words. See that nothing
remains in your conscious mind save a naked intent stretching
out toward God.' "

She pauses and sips from a water glass, and she is surprised to see that the sisters have stopped eating and are peering at her with affection, disfavor, or fascination, as if there are
hidden meanings to be augured from the book's pages just
because it is she who is reading them.

She looks down at the next sentence but hot tears blur it.
She tries to think but cannot. She hears silence and embarrassment, and then after a while she hears Mother Saint-Raphaël
announce "*Satis*" and Mariette goes down among them again.

New Year's Eve. Mass of Saint Sylvester, Pope, Confessor.

Chapter. Just beyond the great doors into the oratory, externs
and novices await Compline with Mariette, saying rosaries or
simply leaning against the hallway walls with their eyes tightly
shut, hearing everything.

In choir, Sister Saint-Pierre is whispering, as always, *"Tout pour Jesus."* She coughs into her habit sleeve and sits honestly upright again.

Sister Saint-Denis gives her great weight to the right arm of her stall and thinks how gorgeously tender and kind Jesus continues to be, untying and gathering her to Himself in a new way through the glorious mystery of His five wounds.

Sister Véronique touches a handkerchief to her sore pink nose. She then fastidiously refolds it and tucks it under the green rubber band on her wrist that also holds a flat pencil.

Sister Marthe scratches a pepper sauce from her thumbnail. She slyly offers it to Sister Saint-Michel, who reddens while trying to hide her giggles.

Sister Félicité tries to spell out the word that Sister Virginie's knuckle is printing surreptitiously on her upper thigh: "Mariette."

Mother Saint-Raphaël uncertainly walks up to the altar of Our Lady of Sorrows and kisses it and turns. She orchestrates the silence for a while before she looks down through half-glasses to her handwritten statement and reads:

"We may have heard our sisters using the word 'stigmata' and not understood them. Well, the word has its origins in the Greek for *tattoo*. Stigmatics are people who bear in their bodies the injuries of Christ's crucifixion. Saint Francis of Assisi is the first person to have been privileged by them, in 1224. A fellow Franciscan wrote of him that 'his hands and feet had as it were piercings made by nails . . . while his side appeared to have been lanced, and blood often trickled therefrom.'

"Some three hundred instances of the phenomenon have been confirmed since then, generally among women and generally among the Catholic religious, although Protestants and unbelievers have been surprised by them, too. We here may have heard of Louise Lateau of Belgium and Anne Catherine Emmerich of Germany, both famous in the century just past for their ecstasies and bleedings. We probably have *not* heard of all those frauds and impostors who impressed Christ's wounds on themselves for their own purposes.

"There was a Scottish philosopher named David Hume who said it is contrary to our experience for miracles to be true, but that it is *not* contrary to our experience for testimony about them to be false. We have all lately heard gossip about peculiar things that have happened here and seem to be miraculous. We may rejoice to have these wondrous deeds in our midst, and yet we cannot forget that we have a hard and fast duty to truth. Wisdom demands of us the prudence and reserve to ask our postulant to explain herself.

"I know that we have not all been persuaded that Mariette did not create or provoke these precious wounds, whether unwittingly or for some ulterior motive. And yet Reverend Marriott and I are agreed in giving no thought to having doctors look at her, for that will only garner us fame, publicity and quarrels. You may be assured, however, that if we find that our postulant is shamming or is so deranged that she could purposely hurt herself, she shall not remain in our haven for one more day. Having said that, we both feel that if these indeed are preternatural gifts from God, then in His giving them to one of ours in the cloister He has gone to great effort to keep the stigmata hidden from the world. In our midst Mariette shall pass the hours unhallowed, unhindered, and unobserved. Shall we disrupt our orderly lives and sabotage God's plan for Mariette and His faithful servants by making everything public?

"Wondrous things do happen here, but they take place amidst great tranquillity. We shall make it our duty to preserve that. We shall try to find a natural explanation for these phenomena if we can, and we shall deny they are holy gifts to Mariette until there is no other alternative. We know there *are* miracles in the gospels, but we show them disrespect if we dispose ourselves to believe in the simply fabulous. And we must keep in mind that there are a good many more pages in holy scripture that show how little pleasure God takes in astounding us with His power. Let us therefore be wary of hallucinations and tricks and whatever seems wonderful or surprising. And let us remember that sainthood has little to do with the preternatural but a great deal to do with the simple day-to-day practice of the Christian virtues."

Mass of the Circumcision of Our Lord.

Cold and calm under mackerel skies that pink in the sunset.

A mother skunk and four kittens find the food in the high, frame compost heap.

Sister Aimée is halfway through *The Book of Privy Counseling* and salt pork is in the stew.

Evening recreation is taken in the haustus room, where Sisters Honoré, Véronique, Philomène, and Saint-Denis perform four concerti by Vivaldi while five or six professed sisters worriedly stare at their postulant.

After Compline, Mariette gets into her nightgown and kneels on the floor to hastily pen another letter, her hand moving with great speed and urgency across the page.

1 January 1907

At this hour when your servants here are at rest and seem to be content in their repose, I find myself enjoying a happiness that the sweetest sleep could not afford me. I have to write to you now, I cannot wait, I have no way of containing these feelings. Hear how my heart speaks to you and hurts for you to reply to it. See how it consecrates to

*you its sleepless hours and its impatience. I have grown
jealous of all who befriend you, yet it is my fondest wish to
find you more admirers. Every thought I have is of you.
Every sentence I speak that is not about you seems empty
and without purpose. Were it necessary to give up all the
worldly pleasures of my life to gain one instant of happiness for you, I would do it without hesitation.*

Mass of Saint Genevieve, Virgin.

Everything but houses and trees are in the great white stomach of winter, and gray doom is in the skies. Externs stand at
their windows in knitted black sweaters and watch as a cruel
wind sharks what it can.

Feast of the Holy Name of Jesus.

Timbers, sawhorses, and hovering dust in a milky chute of
sunlight.

Chisel and adze and some sixpenny nails thorning a green
tarpaulin.

Sister Marie-Madeleine hunkers in a jean carpenter's
apron as she nudges an oak plank a half-inch on a floor joist
and then hammers a nail flush to the wood with five hard
damning blows.

Sisters Geneviève and Léocadie are in the scriptorium
composing histories of Trent for their course in ecclesiology.
Sister Geneviève is getting a footnote when she sees a house
spider with long legs as delicate as hairs tentatively walk sideways onto an open book, and she uses her pencil to slowly
chase it this way and that on the page.

*   *   *

A gardener's ladder is angled against the freshly painted refectory wall, and Sister Véronique is in difficult balance as she prints above the fifth window in beautiful calligraphy, "Eat and drink that which is offered to you. Luke 10:7."

Mariette is carrying six gray blankets in the hallway when she woozily tilts against a wall and skids forward until Sister Monique puts down her floor mop and hurries to her. And Mariette is white as paper when she looks up and faintly says, "Will you please take me to Jesus? I need him."

"Shall we go to the Blessed Sacrament?"

"Yes; please."

Keeping her upright by her left elbow, Sister Monique helps the postulant to the oratory. Halfway there, Mariette slackens to her knees and shyly looks up. "Oh, Sister, I'm so ashamed!"

"You're ill."

"No," she whispers. "Look at my hands."

Blood is trickling down the front of her habit, and her hands are red with fresh wounds.

Mass of the Epiphany of Our Lord.

Second rising.

Sister Catherine hears the first of the three psalms of the Hour as she hunches over the dresser in the priest's sacristy, fastidiously laying out his white chasuble and stole and maniple for Mass, and putting atop them his underthings, the white-tasseled cincture and ankle-length alb and the hood that is called an amice. She pours Sister Antoinette's own red wine from a gunnysacked bottle into a fancy glass cruet and fills its twin with fresh snow water before taking the pair to an Empire table beside the high altar. Easing down to the Communion rail, she unlatches it and half genuflects and without haste walks down the main aisle to the narthex in order to open the great doors for the half-dozen villagers who generally attend Mass on holy days.

And she is astonished to see that in spite of the darkness and the earliness of the hour, thirty people or more have been patiently waiting outside the church, and six press forward to hand her charlotte russe in a copper mold and jars of sweet-meats and preserves.

"Oh, you are too kind!" Sister Catherine says.

And a Czech woman asks, "Is she there?"

An hour later, at Holy Communion, Père Marriott holds a gold ciborium in his hand as he goes down the three steps from the high altar to the great oaken grille, where Sister Catherine unfastens the half door above the oratory Communion rail. Each sister stands prayerfully with folded hands and floor-lowered eyes until her turn has come, and then she kneels to receive Christ in the Host. And as the prioress and professed sisters are replaced at the rail by the externs and novices and Mariette kneels for Holy Communion, Père Marriott hears the shoe noise of people in the church behind him hurrying up the side aisles or shifting positions in their pews in order to catch a fresh glimpse of the famous postulant. And she cries with shame as she receives the Host, then stands and hides her face in her bandaged hands.

Mass of Saint Baldwin, Martyr.

Jan. 10th, 1907

My dear Sisters:

May the grace of Our Lord Jesus Christ be with you all.

We pray that the sisters below will talk confidenti-

ally to Reverend Marriott in Mother Superior's rooms on matters pertaining to the postulant, Mariette Baptiste:

Sister Catherine, Sister Saint-Pierre, Sister Agnès, Sister Saint-Denis, Sister Philomène, Sister Geneviève, Sister Hermance.

Everyone else is invited to write their impressions of our postulant so that the spirits of good or evil that have moved her here may be truly discerned and her progress in Christian perfection may be determined.

Your, poor in holiness,
Mother Saint-Raphaël

Sister Philomène hurries down to the visitation parlor next to the prioress's suite but halts her stride just outside the door and humbly enters. Elderly Sister Catherine is sitting there on the forward few inches of a tapestried Empire chair and hissing the rosary prayers in half-whispered French.

"*Benedicite,*" Sister Philomène says.

"*Dominus.*"

Sister Catherine holds out her ear as Sister Philomène tries, "*Je suis après toi, je pense.*" I am after you, I think. And then Sister Marguerite is behind her. "*Soeur Catherine?*"

She smiles. "*Maintenant?*" Now?

Sister Philomène helps her up and ineptly walks her to the prioress's suite. And when the door is closed, Sister Philomène hears Père Marriott saying, "*Nous parlerons en français s'il vous plaît.*" We'll speak in French if you like.

"*Anglais serait pénible pour moi.*" English would be hard for me.

Sister Philomène holds her hands tight to her ears as she waits her turn in the hallway.

Mass of Saint Hyginus, Pope, Martyr.

Mariette is in the scriptorium at the twelve-person library table, hurriedly sketching on the blank sides of a hundred used papers. She no sooner finishes a sketch than she hates it and hits it aside and with great fury tries another. Her hands are pink and raw with household work. Where just a few days ago there were blood-red holes she could hide a penny in, there are now only faint and tender healings and soon these, too, will go away.

Sister Pauline has been assigned the task of observing the postulant, but she is too uneasy for reading and too cold just sitting there, so she gets up and stares down into the garden through the pitted and frosted windowpanes. She sees Sister Honoré in a tattered black coat and head shawl and mittens, slowly traveling the shoveled sidewalks as she says the rosary to herself. Each prayer grayly feathering from her mouth.

Sister Pauline turns and sashays toward Mariette. She lifts up one sketch and another and she then looks at twenty other sketches littering the great table and floor. Each drawing, she thinks at first, is exactly the same: just two intensely sad and masculine ink-black eyes set underneath a hint of ink-black brows. Looking more carefully, though, she recognizes slight differences and intricate changes in emphasis. Sincerity in one shades into harsh judgment in another, just as sympathy gives way to trouble or affection or a kind of innerness that may be understanding. And then she is aware of Mariette's awareness and she sees in Mariette's eyes what she's seen in the sketches. Tears.

Feast of the Holy Family.

Sunday, just after Sext, Mariette is told she's to go to the visitation parlor and she does so.

Dr. Baptiste is there in his sea otter automobile coat, his hands in his suit pants pockets, staring out at six crows in the churchyard gleaning Sister Anne's squander of popcorn.

She says nothing as she stands a few feet from the grille, but gradually he senses her presence and turns and stares for half a minute. "I heard," he says.

"We aren't supposed to have our parents here now."

"Mother Saint-Raphaël sent a note."

"She shouldn't make exceptions."

Dr. Baptiste smiles. "You are *exceptionnelle.*"

"Are you in good health, Papa?"

Shrugging, he sits down on a green tapestried chair and gives his ruddy cheek to his left fist. She can smell Murad cigarette tobacco floating from his black suit coat. She can see the shine of brilliantine on his great mustache. "*Your* health is the question, Mariette."

"Please don't think about it."

"Just let me look at your hands."

She hides them behind her back.

"Are they bleeding still?"

She dully shakes her head.

"Are they healed?"

"Yes."

"Well then, let me see how that is done."

"No, Papa."

"Examining them won't hurt."

"Christ has forbidden them to science."

Her father frowns with irritation at Mariette and says, "You are talking idiotically."

"I have said what I have to say," she says. "We love you, Papa." And she goes.

Mass of Saint Anthony of Egypt, Abbot.

Sisters Claudine, Saint-Luc, Saint-Michel, and Zélie hood themselves in shawls and tightly button riding coats over their cardigan sweaters and then go out through the horse pasture with fishing poles and tackle until they can mince onto the green mirror of ice on the river.

Every now and then sisters pause in the eastward hallway to thrillingly watch the fisherwomen hunkering on the ice. And every now and then they hear a yell of joy as a line is hauled up and a waggling green perch is held so the others can praise it.

Sext is prayed outdoors and dinner is skipped. And only when snowflakes as big as postage stamps begin fluttering down at nightfall do the sisters trudge indoors with their catch and heave twelve fish up on the scullery table. "We all think you're very brave," Sister Véronique says, and Sister Saint-Luc grins redly as she holds her hands to a stove.

And Mariette stares with fascination as Sister Dominique heedlessly hammers her cleaver down, chopping the fish heads from their bodies, and the perch stay alive for a little while, their gills still seeking what they're used to, their mouths slowly opening and closing as if trying to say what they're seeing.

She was always below me in choir, and she knelt with her attention fixed the whole time on Christ in the tabernacle, quite insensible to all other things but that. We'd have Mass or the Hours and there would be sisters who were so moved by her devotion that they would ask to be remembered in prayer. She did not seem to see or hear them. Often I undertook to reply, assuring them that I would communicate their requests to Mariette. And I would.

With Mariette I feel a sense of quiet. Merely seeing her in meditation makes me recollected and patient, and it gives me great consolation and strength, and I do not feel so much the heavy weight of my cares. What an account we here must all give to God if we do not appreciate the gift He has given us in sending this angelic girl to our house!

*   *   *

She thinks she's better than us you can tell. She's always putting on airs and being so high and mighty, especially with us Externs. Sr. Anne says that's against the Rules! She's lied about a hundred things, not just this. She gets up close to windows at night so she can admire her pretty self like in mirrors. And I smelt perfume on her too. You ask me about her and I'll tell you plenty.

You cannot look her in the face for she seems a seraph; when you have observed this holy postulant for a while, you are humbled by her purity and faith. She prefers to be alone now, and is more silent, more serious than heretofore, but she still takes part in her kitchen and housekeeping work as of old. At prayer she appears to be perpetually in ecstasy. If you saw her as I do, you too would be moved to tears. Would that we all could hear the voice and see the visions that have been bestowed on that darling child!

I shall never believe in these fantasies and I have commanded her in prayer to shun whatever extraordinary manifestations hinder her progress in the ordinary way of devout life. We have had entirely too much mysticism here and too little mortification.

Of Mariette I can only say that the most wonderful phenomena are continually happening to her as has happened only to our hallowed saints in the past. In her I seem to behold someone not of this world. Oh, what a happiness to have had such a blessed woman amongst us! I, for one, can affirm that the whole time Mariette has been here, never once has the tiniest trouble arisen in the sisterhood on her account, nor did I ever notice any defect in her, I say no defect, not even the smallest.

Mass of Saint Agnes, Virgin, Martyr.

Waking from a troubled sleep, she turns to her side on her palliasse and is surprised that her door is open. She hears nothing in the Great Silence and then she hears hitched breathing. Everything is shaded and hidden and black. And yet she knows there are four there. She can feel herself being seen and changed and imagined.

She prays as she sees the gray blanket being tugged away, but she is too frightened to so much as lift her head. She tries to still her hammering heart; she tries not to breathe. And then she's fiercely pressed down to the palliasse and miseried by hands. Even her mouth is covered. She can't scream or wrestle from the harsh kisses and pressures and hate and insistence. Hands haul her nightgown as high as her thighs and hoist it underneath her haunches. She prays as her knees are held wide. Horrible pictures are put in her head.

Everything stops at that point. Abruptly. Eventually she opens her eyes. She is alone in the room and the door is closed. Silence is the only presence.

She thinks, *You were dreaming.*

And then she thinks, *No. I was not.*

Mass of Saint Raymond of Pennafort, Confessor.

She helps Sister Catherine after Mixt, washing the green marble of the high altar with a milk of powdered chalk and pumice and common soda, then tenderly drying it as if it were Christ's body. And she is reverently laying out a fresh altar cloth of steam-ironed nainsook and Alençon lace when Sister Catherine hesitantly touches her wrist and Mariette turns to see Sister Félicité giving the handsigns *You, go, talk, priest.* Mariette genuflects and follows Sister Félicité into the oratory and out to the hallway and the prioress's suite.

Sister Marguerite is hunched over a stack of fine writing paper at Mother Superior's desk and exactingly filling a green fountain pen from a jar of India ink. And Mother Saint-Raphaël is seriously presiding from the pink velvet sofa and staring at the postulant in an assaying way, with a tray of the sister's testimonies under her ivory hands.

"*Benedicite*," Mariette says, and curtsies.

"*Dominus*," the prioress says. She graciously indicates a wide plush chair, and Mariette sits as she's been taught, just on the front, her back as vertical as a bookend, facing a tall window of twelve shining panes that shimmer the high wall outside and the fruit trees glazed with ice.

"You know why you're here, Mariette?"

"Yes, Reverend Mother."

"Sister Marguerite is just writing down what we say. She's under pain of serious sin not to repeat what she hears. You should try to remember that whatever you say is for others and you may need to further clarify what is to us only too clear."

"Yes, Reverend Mother."

Half a minute passes, and Mother Saint-Raphaël explains, "We are waiting for Père Marriott." She watches as Sister Marguerite uses tongs to clatter four chunks of coal into the heater. She watches her shut the iron door and dotingly sit again. She squints mistrustfully at Mariette as she asks, "Don't you frankly find it a tremendous surprise that Christ would choose *you* of all people for these ecstasies?"

"Yes, I do."

"Why?"

"I have been a terrible sinner."

Mother Saint-Raphaël stares at Mariette as if she has become an intricate sentence no one can understand. "Saint Philip Neri commenced his interview of a presumed ecstatic by asking just that question. She got very angry and grandly told the priest why she was in such great favor with God.

Saint Philip promptly halted the interview, knowing that the woman's pride showed that she wasn't special at all."

"We are all special to God."

"Of course," Mother Saint-Raphaël says. "And you need not educate me on the catechism." She heels over to find her walking cane and heaves herself up to her feet just as Sister Anne faintly raps on the door and Père Marriott hurries in. Mariette rises with Sister Marguerite, and all half curtsy to him as Père Marriott heats his hands underneath his arms and smiles at each fawning woman.

"Are we prepared, Reverend Mother?" he asks.

"We are."

The old priest hitches a green wing chair around until it is just opposite Mariette, and he tentatively settles into it before tilting toward her and admitting, "I have so looked forward to this!"

"Talking?" Mariette asks.

"Certainly! I have become so curious!"

She is embarrassed by his benevolence and grandfatherly interest, and she blushes as she smiles. She hears Mother Saint-Raphaël say, "She is expected for Sext," but Père Marriott does not turn to the old prioress until a half-second after she's gone. And then he faces Mariette again and gladly asks, "Shall we begin?"

Mass of the Conversion of Saint Paul.

Méridienne. Sisters Léocadie and Geneviève and Hermance and Claudine are huddling around Mariette and harrying her with talk as they wade through high snow in gutta-percha galoshes. Excitement makes their voices shrill.

Mariette tries not hearing for the hour and she rests her seeing on the whiteness. Haystacks have softened into breasts. The horsetail grass is hooded. Everywhere they walk they are tearing holes in the snow.

She finds the Host in the grieving gray skies overhead and then sees a boy in a green mackinaw coat surging through the high snow at the pasture fence fifty yards away. She sees him using both hands to wave at her when she turns away, and he is shouting phrases that a hard wind tears apart as she walks back to the priory. The sisters stand still for half a minute and then follow Mariette inside.

Septuagesima Sunday.

Méridienne. While Sister Marguerite shares hot barley tea with friends in the chapter room, Mariette sits at a library table in the scriptorium and concentrates on a great variety of holy relics that are arrayed before her like runes.

"Just try," Sister Hermance says.

She sheepishly smiles and peers at a tooth. "Whose is this?"

"Mine," Sister Félicité says.

"Whose tooth, I meant."

"Oh. Saint Valentine."

She judges it again and says, "I'm sorry, but it isn't."

"But is it holy?"

She regards Sister Félicité with regret. "It's not even human."

"She might be wrong," Sister Geneviève says, but Sister Félicité holds the tooth tightly inside her hand for a while and then hurries from the room.

Mariette handles a torn inch of yellowed hem and flatly says, "I have no idea."

Sister Véronique hints, "*Sainte Jeanne Françoise de Chantal.*"

Mariette shrugs and says in the higher song of French that she just doesn't know.

Sister Philomène shades that by saying, "*Peut-être.*" Perhaps. And Sister Véronique kisses the hem.

Sister Marthe insists, "Touch mine."

Mariette hears the neediness in Sister Marthe's voice and gets up from the library table. "Everything else is real."

Sister Pauline asks skeptically, "Are they truly?"

"Yes," she says. "I think so."

Sister Sabine is jubilant. "I have a portion of the true cross!"

Mariette considers the milkmaid with sadness, but says, "Yes. You do."

Père Henri Marriott
Our Lady of Sorrows Convent
Arcadia, New York

1 February 1907

My dear Jerome,

Your letter tries so hard to be kind, but behind it I fear I perceive your disdain for my wonderful news about our postulant. Even now I can hear you scoffing. Well, my friend, I too would be incredulous, but like Thomas I have beheld her hands and side and heard what she has said and I have faith in her now as one who may honestly say, Ego stigmata Domini Jesu in corpore meo porto.

She was sitting at table with me just yesterday. She being in ecstasy. Experimentally, I put one of my breviaries in front of her and we recited the prayers alternately. Even though she has scant Latin, she read the lessons of the nocturns and answered the responsories and versicles with admirable exactness, turning over the pages regularly. She was quite insensible to the heat of a match when I held it close to her shining eyes. She was not shocked or pained when I tapped her flesh with a pin. And then, radiant and joyous, she came out of ecstasy. What a wonderful impression she made upon me! And how short that half-hour

seemed! We mortals have such a great hunger for super-
natural things.

She shrinks from being touched, and from the most
innocent caresses. Even her father has not been permitted
to kiss her since she was thirteen. Does one say she's neu-
rotic, then, or is she simply chaste? I shall prefer the latter,
for she is in all things humble, charming, loveable, full of
fidelity and charity, truly one for whom it is her confessor's
duty merely to "dust off the wings." And yet she is so natural that one would have a hard time differentiating her
from any healthy young woman. To treat with her, to
labor in helping her to worthily correspond to the blessed
impulses of divine grace does not tax me, as so often happens, but rather gives me intense satisfaction. I have spoken
to her for many hours on heavenly things without feeling
the time pass. She seems to find some difficulty in replying
to philosophical questions I have put to her; still what she
says is so much to the point, so wise and full of unction that
it is enchanting to listen to her. I heave a sigh now as I tell
of her.

Is this all a phantasy? Am I dealing with a holy young
woman's delusions? We know how susceptible the religious
are. Even me! We are bored and dull and tired of each
other, and we have such a yearning for some sign from
God that this matters, that our prayers and good works are
important to Him. Is she preying upon that? Is she trying to
entertain?

I have so many questions and I have too little science,
but in my reading I have found that the heightened pas-
sions of hysterics promote a general irascibility. Hence it
happens that persons afflicted with this malaise often become insupportable to those who associate with them.
Quite to the contrary, our M. is demure and calm beyond
measure, quiet in company and tranquilly smiling. Evil

spirits have been assailing her, or so she says, in a hundred horrible and threatening forms, but she neither dwells on them nor shows fanciful signs of fear. She is being praised abundantly by the sisters but is not puffed up, nor do suspicions and abuse disturb her. She is a perfect model of equanimity. And yet she is a challenge to our theology, psychology, medicine. God would have it so many times in our human history. He is never at variance with Himself, only with our meager understanding of Him.

Well, I have given you much to think about, Jerome, and a great many reasons to write, so please be quick about it. You and your holy sister and mother have often been in my thoughts and are presented to Heaven in all my Masses, as I dare say I may have been in yours. How else to explain the benefices I have received of late? The book, as the saying goes, hangs fire, but I shall try to send you pages in a fortnight or so. And tell me more about your trip—the horrible ship's food and the opera and Otto K. and our beloved Louvain. Was Clermont perchance there? I do hope so, and that you have further information about the pontiff. Europe is so far away.

Pax Christi,
Marriott

Mass of the Purification of the Blessed Virgin Mary.

Hundreds of people have come for Sunday Mass and have put before the high altar horseshoe geraniums, hothouse flowers, a box of parboiled rabbits, green ferns in a Wardian case, a fancy-worked purple table scarf of Java canvas and silesia, a handmade Aeolian harp, ginger biscuits, huckleberry cake, Ottawa root beer, an old Shetland shawl, a blue ornamental hassock, and a harness dressed in glycerine and tallow.

At Holy Communion half the church is huddled up by the front pews and railing to have a glimpse of the postulant in the north choir behind the grille. She is not in her stall, however, but has hidden herself from the public and is getting up from Sister Claudine's kneeler in the south choir. Tears of shame and penance shiver like hot mercury in her eyes as she finally kneels before Père Marriott, and then there are sighs and talk and great noise from the people until she gets up again and turns away to the oratory without lifting a hand in blessing, and then Père Marriott goes down to his parishoners with the Hosts and a haughty woman squats to reach through the railing and take back her jar of quince marmalade.

Sexagesima Sunday.

Six people in old pelt coats are trying to hide from the bitter cold as they scurry toward the church in the predawn darkness. Another four are a half-mile behind them. And horses are splashing through pasture snow in front of full sleighs and toboggans.

Sister Anne is on the church steps in a gray sweater and galoshes, flirting up fresh snow with a broom and saying nothing even to old friends as she opens the church doors. And Sisters Sabine and Zélie are up on high stepladders inside, just finishing hooking up a great purple theater curtain across the front of the grille as Sister Honoré sings from the Psalter. Some people wait a half hour for the great curtain to part, and then they get up from the pews with irritation and go out into the night again.

Mass of Saint Andrew Corsini, Bishop.

Sister Véronique is a half hour late in joining the novices for their weekly art lesson after Nones, and she finds division is invading them just as it has the older professed. Each sits morosely in a high-backed chair with her sketch pad and pencil and adamant opinion about Mariette, and is hot, solitary, taciturn, *triste*, watchful, high-strung, discontent. Tears flow from Sister Hermance, and Sister Léocadie's cheeks are as redly blotched as if she's recently been slapped. And when Mariette walks in from a talk with Père Marriott, Sister Philomène is so overpowered that she rushes up and fleetingly kisses her and temperamentally flees the room, Sister Hermance just behind her.

Mass of Saint Agatha, Virgin, Martyr.

Sister Saint-Estèphe is surprised from her sleep when she hears heavy furniture screech across the flooring not too far away. She rushes out into the hallway in just her white nightgown and a gray robe hanging open and she thinks she'll be joined by others as she hustles down to Mariette's cell, but Sister Saint-Estèphe is alone there and her left hand rakes back the graying froth of her hair as she fearfully puts her ear to the door.

She hears flesh smack against a wall. She hears hoarse breathing and heaves and hard, masculine effort. She tries the door latch but can do no more than rattle it.

Wrestling noises seem to roam the room, and the postulant's tin basin rings as it's flung against a ceiling joist. And yet Mariette is silent. Every now and then she pants or whimpers with pain, and then Sister Saint-Estèphe hears a greater noise as she imagines the postulant being hurled onto her palliasse and falling onto the floor.

Sister Saint-Estèphe hurriedly crosses herself and prays, "Holy Michael defend us in battle, by our protection against the wickedness and snares of the Devil." She hears hitting sounds in the cell, and she shouts over the increasing noise,

"May God rebuke him we humbly pray! And may the prince of the heavenly host, by the power of God, thrust into hell Satan and all the evil spirits who wander through the world seeking the ruin of souls!"

And then there is sudden quiet.

—And you opened the door?

—Sister Marthe did. At first I was afraid to touch it. The Devil and all.

—Sister Marthe heard you yelling?

—And Sister Saint-Luc. Yes.

—But it was only you who went inside.

—Yes, Father. Too scared, the others.

—Well?

—She wasn't bleeding, but her face was horrible. She'd lost every trace of beauty. Oh, I felt so ill for her! She was kneeling there on the floor all bruised and red like he'd hit her a hundred times. And her clothes were half off her like there'd been hounds tearing at them.

—And you say her window was open?

—Like it was the hottest day in July.

—Anyone there could have got out that way, yes?

—Well, I don't know.

—Why did you presume that you heard the Devil inside?

—She said so.

—She could have made those noises herself.

—You ought to just live in this cloister for one night, Father. You'd know the Devil's up to his mischief. You can hear sisters pacing, crying out in their sleep. Everyone's on edge.

—We thank you, Sister.

—She's got me so spooked now!

—Of course.

—We never had wildness like that here before.

Mass of Saint Dorothy, Virgin, Martyr.

Père Marriott is holding confessions during meditation and is hunting a page in his breviary when he hears a sister hastily kneel behind the iron grille. Even before he blesses her, though, he hears her talking. "Oh, I am so afraid," she whispers, and he thinks it's Sister Zélie, then Sister Saint-Stanislas. "We're in league together. She said it was just going to be a theatrical, but it's gotten out of hand. And now she knows that I'll tell and she'll hurt me."

Every sentence slightly changes in tone, as if she were trying to disguise her sultry voice. Sister Geneviève? Sister Claudine? "You're talking about Mariette?"

"She stole things from the infirmary. Chemicals and instruments. When she was taking care of Mother Céline. And she's good at science. She got it from her father. Everything else is from the Devil."

"You are saying this has all been a prank?"

"Worse that that, a cruel deception."

She's poisonous. She's fabricating. She stinks with jealousy and hate. And yet Marriott finds himself asking her, "Does Mariette have a reason?"

"Attention at first. She was just bored. But now she wants to be thought a great saint so she can have her way and get back at us."

He thinks how Mariette smiles as he blesses her. And he sees her pretty form as she kneels at his prie-dieu and softly prays the fifty-first psalm. She turns and blushes and puts the book as it was.

His hands are cold; his inner ear rings; his face, he knows, is white. Marriott tilts on the hard bench and gives influence to his breathing until his faintness passes. "Shall we talk about you now, Sister?" he asks. "Are you here to confess?"

She hisses, "She's in your dreams, isn't she, priest. Oh,

how you sicken her! You should hear the tales she tells. She hates all of us, but especially you. Every day she's been here is a lie."

In his shock he doesn't think to ascertain who it is until he hears her stand up, and when he touches the purple silk curtain aside he sees that the confessional is empty and she is back in the priory.

Mass of Saint Apollonia, Virgin, Martyr.

Examination of conscience and Compline. Everyone tries not to stare at the postulant as she prays. And then the sisters walk two by two from the oratory in the Great Silence, singing "*Ubi Caritas*," Sister Pauline holding a fluttering candle high against the darkness as they go down the hallways. Mariette steps aside just as Sister Emmanuelle does and both touch their holy water stoups as they pass into their cells.

Mariette undoes her black headscarf and slides from her sandals and stands on the cold punishment of the floor as she unfastens her habit and sees the gray mist of her breath softly translated into night.

And sudden as affliction, Sister Honoré is there, holding her in a harrowing stare as she shuts the door and sets down a tallow candle in a dish. She whispers, "You show me your *wounds!*"

Mariette retreats a step without speaking and Sister Honoré throws a hand over Mariette's mouth and tilts her back against the writing desk as she tears at the windings of bloodstained cloth on the postulant's hands, whispering that she'll put a stop to this foolishness, that she's sick of Mariette playing the saint when half the convent knows she's lying.

Mariette handsigns, *Wait*, and Sister Honoré halts the throttling as Mariette first frees her hands and then her feet and gets out of the habit before walking undressed inside the ring of golden candlelight.

—And I saw nothing.

—She was completely naked?

—Yes. And yet there was no blood, no wheals or scars or bruises of any kind. She might have been a virgin bride on her wedding night, she seemed so pretty and faultless and embarrassed.

—You told her what you saw?

—Yes. And she looked at me with such great pity! And she gave me that sweet, forgiving smile as if it was *my* religious faith that was in question, as if Christ or the Devil had blinded me and I ought to be ashamed.

—You weren't, Sister Honoré?

—Well, I felt awkward and lewd just then, but I'm proud that I have exposed her and changed some people's minds.

Mass of Saint Scholastica, Virgin.

2/10/07

My Dear Father Marriott:

Word has reached us here about your involvement in this foolish affair with Mariette Baptiste, whom I know exceedingly well. Have nothing more to do with her. Unsay all you have said. It is useless even to try to unmask her. I have come to know from intimates of hers that what is supposedly happening to Mariette is, as one would suspect, mere hypocrisy and deceit. She is enraptured by the devil and whatever your efforts, they will be to no avail. You should no longer interest yourself in her behalf and advise that mother superior of hers to act in the same manner. You would do well, in fact, to promptly expel her from the priory, for she has no vocation, no purity, no respect for the Church and the sacraments. The high esteem I held Mariette in has now turned to hatred and revulsion. She has a deceived and deceiving soul and will cause irreparable spiritual ruin if she is not shamed and sent away from there. She does not need your assistance, and the Church does not need the ridicule she will open it to. Take it from one who knows her all too well and try not to believe any of these things she says are true. The beauty of her lying is that she herself is so oblivious to it. Were it up to me I would immediately wash my hands of the actress and submit the whole matter to your bishop, and above all I would see to it that she didn't take Holy Communion.

Yours sincerely,
A Worried Priest

—Have you seen the letter?

—Yes.

—Are you troubled by it?

—No.

—Have you any idea who may have sent it?

—The Devil.

—Simple as that.

—In this case, yes.

Mass of the Apparition of Our Lady of Lourdes.

Whispers of pellet snow on the ice.

Late morning. A half rim of moon is faint in a mica-blue sky.

Winter shag blows as a Morgan horse roughs his hoary jaw against a water trough and grandly suffers the zero cold.

A gray and white cat cautiously steps down from a roof

peak and settles against a chimney stack, its paws turned primly underneath its breast.

Sister Geneviève is in a poor-box overcoat as she totters up from a shack with both hands on a heavy tin pail of coal.

Sisters Monique, Virginie, and Antoinette are sipping hot barley tea in the infirmary after an hour in the weather trying to repair the screw on a hundred-year-old winepress.

Window glass over the priest's sink is hatched and helixed with frost but sunshine is bristling on the shellacked window-sill and on a tarnished spoon, a green tin matchbox, and a stoppered chemist's phial holding brown flakes of dried blood. Eighth-inch lettering on the glass tube reads American Pharmaceutical.

Ever so slowly the flakes ooze and redden until the phial holds blood again.

Mariette walks a toweled broom along a hallway by Sister Virginie's cell and then kneels below a horrid crucifixion that she hates, Christ's flesh-painted head like a block of woe, his black hair sleek as enamel and his black beard like ironweed, his round eyes bleary with pity and failure, and his frail form softly breasted and feminine and redly willowed in blood. And yet she prays, as she always does, *We adore you, O Christ, and we praise you, because by your holy cross you have redeemed the world.* And just then, she'll later tell Père Marriott, she is veiled in Christ's blessing and tenderness, she feels it flow down from her head like holy oil and thrill her skin like terror. Everything she has ever wished for seems to have been, in a hidden way, this. Entire years of her life are instantly there as if she could touch any hour of them, but she now sees Jesus present in her history as she hadn't before, kindness itself and everlastingly loyal, good father and friend and husband to her, hurting just as she hurt at times, pleased by her tiniest pleasures, wholly loving her common humanness and her essential uniqueness, so that the treacheries and sins and affronts of her past seem hideous to her and whatever good she's done seems as nothing compared to the shame she feels for her fecklessness and indifference to him. And she is kneeling there in misery and sorrow when she opens her hands like a book and sees an intrusion of blood on both palms, pennies of skin turning redder and slowly rising up in blisters that in two or three minutes tear with the terrible pain of hammered nails, and then the hand flesh jerks with the fierce sudden weight of Christ's body and she feels the hot burn in both wrists. She feels her feet twisted behind her as both are transfixed with nails and the agony in both soles is as though she's stood in the rage of orange, glowing embers. She is breathless, she thirsts, she chills with loss of blood, and she hears Sister Dominique from a great distance, asking "Are you ill?" when she feels an iron point rammed hard against her heart and she faints.

Hours later Mother Saint-Raphaël thinks it important that the most worshipful sisters see the postulant as she is and not as she is being imagined, so just after Vespers twelve of them slowly walk one by one through the infirmary and stare down at Mariette in infatuation and fear and relief as she stares up in a trance and seems to smile at their procession, and Sister Aimée permits them to softly touch Mariette's wrapped hands. Many ask if she is feeling much pain and Sister Aimée replies that the hurt must be excruciating. Each of them who asks for prayers is promised that she'll be remembered just as soon as Mariette wakes up.

And when all the sisters have walked through and Sister Aimée has been excused, Mother Saint-Raphaël installs a stool beside the headrail and with no more than a whisper of sound sits down beside Mariette and is as still as a picture for a while, as composed as a book of ritual, disarray's opposite, her handsome face neutral, her hard sandals flat on the floor, a hand gently inside a hand, intensely watching Mariette as the girl seems to hear harmonies inside her, as she seems to hover outside time. "Mariette?" Mother Saint-Raphaël finally asks. "Are you here now? Are you listening?"

She sees Mariette's dark lashes flutter a little, as if she's breathed over a candle flame. She pets a wisp of sable-brown hair away from the postulant's forehead and says, "It's Mother Saint-Raphaël. Your prioress."

Silver daggers of light shine in Mariette's blue irises and her mouth twitches slightly, as if she's heard and is trying to talk. The prioress is silent, then turns and twists hot water from a washrag and drags it frankly and affectionately over the postulant's too-white face, just as if she were suddenly blind and learning Mariette with her hands. Eventually Mariette opens her eyes.

"Was it the same this time?" the prioress asks.

Mariette thinks. "Yes."

"You were dwelling on Christ's passion."

She agrees.

Mother Saint-Raphaël bestows the washrag to a dish behind her and floats her manly, twisted hands atop her thighs. "Were you alone?"

"Yes."

"Was that necessary, do you think?"

Mariette looks at her carefully, in the half wince of a pianist newly hearing the flaw in one key. "We find God in stillness and silence."

"I'm sorry," Mother Saint-Raphaël says. "I may have added a nuance I didn't intend."

Mariette hurtfully gets up to a sitting position and holds her wrapped hands just below her heart. She smiles understandingly as she says, "And yet you're suspicious still, aren't you."

"I have been troubled by God's motives for this," the prioress says. "I see no possible reasons for it. Is it so Mariette Baptiste will be praised and esteemed by the pious? Or is it so she shall be humiliated and jeered at by skeptics? Is it to honor religion or to humble science? And what are these horrible wounds, really? A trick of anatomy, a bleeding challenge to medical diagnosis, a brief and baffling injury that hasn't yet, in six hundred years, changed our theology or our religious practices. Have you any idea how disruptive you've been? You are awakening hollow talk and half-formed opinions that have no place in our priory, and I have no idea why God would be doing this to us. To you. I do know that the things the villagers have been giving us have not helped us in our vow of poverty. And all the seeking people who have been showing up have not helped our rule of enclosure. And there are breaches to our vow of obedience whenever you become the topic."

She sees that the postulant is staring at her impassively, with a hint, even, of amusement. She says in a sterner way, "I flatter myself that I have been extremely tolerant and patient, thus far. I have done so out of respect for your late sister, and in sympathy for the torment you have in her loss. But I shall not suffer your confusions much longer. And so I pray, Mariette, that if it is in your power to stop this—as I presume it is—that you do indeed stop it." She pauses and then stands. "And if it is in your power to heal me of the hate and envy I have for you now, please do that as well."

Mass of the Seven Holy Founders of the Servites,
Confessors.

12 February 1907

Esteemed Reverend Marriott:

We the undersigned are of the firmest opinion that our blessed priory is being held hostage to a postulant's wiles

and chicanery! We shall not have our convent contami-
nated by her! We shall not tolerate the favoritism and
particular affection shown her thus far! We believe she
possesses not one iota of orthodoxy and we beseech you, for
the good of the younger souls here and for the future of our
holy Church, to have her presented to a proper tribunal
where, our prayers have assured us, her guile and strata-
gems will be found out. Although we harbor no ill feelings
toward our saintly Mother Superior, we do have long
memories and know that such as Mariette were quite
readily dispatched by those glorious emissaries of God's
will whose venerable portraits now grace the halls of our
Motherhouse. We therefore beg of you to conquer the per-
missiveness and infirmity that is so rampant here and treat
this hoax with the thoroughness and gravity it warrants.

Yours in humility,
Sr. Monique, Sr. Saint-Estèphe, Sr. Marthe, Sr. Honoré,
Sr. Marguerite, Sr. Saint-Stanislas, Sr. Félicité, Sr. Aimée

Ash Wednesday.

Sister Zélie wanders down the hallway, drawling four fingers
along the white wall, and then halting outside Mariette's cell,
just as she knew she would. She hesitates and then goes inside
and delights at being there, her callused hands softly touching
down on the furniture as she might have rested them on the
silken heads of infants. Everything is orderly, neat as a pin.
She is pleased to smooth the gray blanket of the palliasse. She
tips a water pitcher and is tempted to drink from it but does
not. She holds a flutter in her stomach as she opens the armoire and presses her face to Mariette's habits, inhaling the
delicious perfume that exudes from them. Sister Zélie is walking toward the secretary when a sandal catches on a finishing

nail that shines from the flooring. She taps the nailhead with her heel and it drops; she kneels in order to pinch the nail, and lifts it without effort from its hole. And then she sees that the floor plank is freed and she furtively tips it up. She crushes her habit sleeve above her elbow and reaches down underneath the flooring to a joist. She pulls out a sheaf of handwritten pages tied up in a red satin ribbon.

She hears the floor creak and finds Mother Saint-Raphaël frowning into Mariette's cell from the hallway. Sister Zélie simpers and holds up the papers. "Look."

I have been told to receive our hundreds of Sunday visitors in the parlor, but all who speak to me think I am insane. My head empties and I do not know how to reply to them. Surely Mother Superior must be demented to think me fit for such duties. I hold no conversations but those I have with you. I have no interest in people unless I see Jesus in them.

Mother Saint-Raphaël has forbidden me Communion for six days now. Oh, how I ache for him, and how tortured and sick and desolate I have felt without him! I grieve to imagine how dull and haggard and ugly his Mariette must seem to him now! And yet I should think myself hateful if being deprived of him for these six days had not grossly disfigured me.

What a cruel mistress I am to complain so much about your absence when I should be wooing you and praising you for your kindnesses and sweet presence. You see, though, that I have become obsessed by you. You are not here with me enough if for one brief moment I have no sense of you. And yet I have only gratitude for the desperation you have caused me, and I loathe the peace in which I lived before I truly knew you.

—Well, there are hundreds more, as you know.

—Writing was a kind of prayer for me.

—Mother Saint-Raphaël was quite displeased. Another postulant may have been sent away.

—But I won't be?

—You have a cult.

At Matins, Sister Marguerite walks down from the choir with a red book and kneels before Mother Saint-Raphaël for a blessing before going to the green marble altar below Our Lady of Sorrows and reading: " *'The Constitution of the Second Order of the Sisters of the Crucifixion in Accordance with the Common Observance of the Rule of Saint Benedict.*

" 'Chapter forty-six. Excommunication for faults.

" 'If our sister is found to be at odds with the Holy Rule, or disobedient to her mother superior's directions, or otherwise detrimental to our way of perfection, she shall be admonished by her prioress in accordance with the Lord's injunction. Even then she may not redress her sins; if this be the case, she shall be reproved in public. If, however, there is still no transformation or amendment in her conduct, she shall be subject to excommunication.

" 'She shall eat alone, when and how much in accordance with whatever the prioress deems proper. She shall not intone a psalm or antiphon or read a lesson in the oratory until she has been corrected. She shall work alone, dwelling with us in penance and sorrow. Eyes shall not communicate with her, she shall not be accompanied, she shall not be spoken to by hand or voice. She is not to be blessed as she passes, nor is her food to be blessed, nor is she to be blessed in common prayers except in pleas that God shall forgive her trespasses.

" 'We hold out hope that these punishments may not bring her condemnation but health in mind and body. Ever mindful, however, of Saint Paul who said, "Put away the evil one from among you," and, "If the faithless one depart, let him depart," the prioress shall finally determine if our wayward sister shall be sent away permanently. We do these things so that one sheep may not infect our flock with her disease.' "

Mass of Saint Valentine, Priest and Martyr.

Sister Aimée strolls behind Mariette as she walks achingly down the hallway in half-mittens and gray wool stockings, a hand holding her side. And then Mariette sees an hourglass and four stacked books just outside her cell, and Sister Zélie folding her black habits into a box. Sisters Sabine and Saint-Michel and Claudine are hauling out her pine armoire and the feet are chattering along the plank floor.

"Are they taking out everything?" Mariette asks.

Sister Claudine hesitantly stares and then continues with her tasks.

Sister Zélie is haphazardly putting white towels into the box while pretending she hasn't heard. Written in the prioress's hand and tacked up on the door is a paper scrap that reads: "She is to be delivered over for the destruction of the flesh, that her spirit may be saved in the day of the Lord. Saint Paul, 1 Corinthians 5:5."

Mariette turns to Sister Aimée, but she knowingly walks down the hallway to a four-by-six closet that held priests' vestments and thuribles and monstrances and homely paintings but is now completely empty save for a holy water stoup and a palliasse rolled up underneath a simple wooden cross.

"You'll be staying here," Sister Aimée says.

"Why?"

"Mother Superior orders it."

"Why here, I mean? Why not some other place?"

Sister Aimée frowns at Mariette's innocence and then she finds the interior door with one hand. Eight tall iron bars firmly clank against an iron lock plate and change the closet into a jail.

Sister Marthe tiredly walks down the hall in the flooding darkness of first rising and pauses to tap the castanets in her hand before whining, "In the name of God, my sisters, let us rise!" She hears four or five of them reciting, "His holy name be praised!" and she proceeds down the hallway as if she were dully reentering sleep. When she passes Mariette's jail cell, however, she cannot resist looking in. She is just there in the corner, undressed still and kneeling on the hard floor like the night terror in a child's closet, her wild brown hair all thrash and storm, her hands hidden behind her back, her stare as serious as torture. She smiles insincerely at Sister Marthe and says, "*Benedicite*," and Sister Marthe hurriedly walks on.

—I have no memories of that.
—You deny it then?
—Each tale I hear is a place I haven't been.

Mass of the Flight into Egypt.

Walking in procession, the sisters go into the tallow-lit refectory for collation, hesitating only to raise their habits slightly and step over Mariette whose penance it is to lie facedown on the dining hall floor, like the shoe-black door to a dark, dank cellar where fruit blooms in the jars.

And at the first rising she is prostrate on the great red Persian carpet as the sisters walk in pairs from the nave and genuflect just short of her and go up into the choirs for Matins and Lauds. Each one tries not to look, and yet each one sees her. She pulls their eyes like the print on a page. She is the stillness that ends their prayers. She is as present to them as God.

Walking nowhere in particular, Sisters Anne, Claudine, and Sabine talk solemnly about their own imperfections and slosh through fresh snow past the stiff, whitened cattails of the marsh and the white paws of the firs, and past the old printery sunk to its sills in snow and weed wrack and wind spew and ruin. And when they sit it's on a stone bench in the cemetery, in the company of forty-one names, including the first Sister Geneviève, a prioress, and another Sister Saint-Michel, born in Amiens, France. Sister Sabine is drawing houses with a stick when she gets the feeling they're being watched, and she turns to see that the postulant is just beside Mother Céline's fresh grave and starkly black against the white stage of the snow and the green curtain of pine woods, but glamorously alone and forlorn like a pretty girl about to sing, and with all the sisters listening.

"Don't look," Sister Sabine says, but they do, and Mariette lifts her hands as if she's written on the palms. Each turns away.

Mass of Saint Gabriel of Our Lady of Sorrows, Confessor.

Mariette in ecstasy.

She's been seated on an ottoman in the chapter room in the Great Silence following Compline, and she's poised there while Sister Philomène and Hermance recruit Sisters Geneviève and Léocadie to confirm their witness. Each approaches Mariette reverently and sits with perfect faith and attention, trying to share in the Christ she is seeing as she stares at a spot just above their heads.

"Where are you?" Sister Philomène whispers.

"Sitting in choir," she says, "with the Psalter."

"And is Jesus there?"

"Yes."

Sister Léocadie asks, "Oh, what does he look like?"

"Handsome," she says.

Sister Hermance hushes her voice while insisting, "You have to tell us what's happening!"

"Christ takes the book," Mariette says, "and sings the psalms in Hebrew, in the high tenor of the cantors, just as he did in his childhood."

She gets up. She walks over to a tallow candle. She pinches out the flame. She goes to another and extinguishes that one, too. Everywhere around her there is darkness. She tells them, "He holds my hand in his and we two walk down the hallway to his house inside ours. Which is his heart."

Sister Philomène turns and sees Mother Saint-Raphaël halted at the door. She worriedly prepares to stand and curtsy, but she sees the prioress bless herself and interestedly sit down in the bleakness farthest away from the postulant.

"What else?" Sister Léocadie asks.

Mariette thinks for a little while and says, "We are alone. We touch each other, but he withdraws. 'You are unclean,' he says, and I am ashamed because I see that it's true. Every sin I have committed is written in ink on my skin. Christ tells me to undress. And then he gently washes me with his hands. With holy water from great earthen jugs heated by the sun."

She pauses. She peers toward Mother Saint-Raphaël as if she's just learned that she's there.

Sister Geneviève flatly says, "We're in suspense, Mariette."

She continues, "We hear a hubbub and noise outside, as in an Eastern bazaar. Hands reach through the windows. Hopeless people walk in and then immediately walk out, as if the house is empty. What sorrow we both feel for them, but it's as if they can't see or hear us. We talk of a great many things, of affliction and faith and the full love of God. Everything he says is put so simply. Every word penetrates me as softly as water entering a sponge. Weeks seem to pass, and yet only a half hour goes by. I know from hearing the choir singing the verses and responsories for Lauds. And he tells me what a great pleasure it is for his father to hear that. All our trying to please him pleases him, Jesus says."

She kneels just in front of the frowning prioress, her half-mittened hands nestled against her habit. She smiles. "And he gives me food as I have never eaten. And fine wine from a jeweled chalice. When he tells me to sleep, I do so at once, and he holds me. And I share in him as if he's inside me. And he is."

Mother Saint-Raphaël firmly purses her mouth and harshly slaps Mariette's face. And then she gets up and goes out.

Mass of Saint John of the Cross.

Collation. A flame trembles in the palm of a used-up candle beside Sister Véronique as she reads the *Lectio Divina* of Saint Ignatius of Antioch's "Epistle to the Romans." And the prioress is drinking plain hot water as she peers across the nighted refectory at Mariette.

She seems hooded and dour and disoriented as she sits with her hands inside her sleeves, not eating, not hearing, hardly there at all. Everything seems dire to the postulant. Every choice seems taken from her. And then Mariette seems to perceive a call and she looks up into the darkness as she slips into another ecstasy, her healed hands rising up from her lap as if she's lifting an offertory, and then freezing there, high above the dining table, as if she's turned to wood.

Everyone stares at Mariette's trance until the prioress interrupts Sister Véronique's reading by irritably shouting, "Wake her!"

Sister Hermance puts down her spoon and tentatively touches Mariette twice.

"Harder."

She gives Mariette a fiercer push but she's firm as furniture to her hand and Sister Hermance appeals to the prioress with the shine of tears in her eyes.

The kitchen workers have come out and when Sister Saint-Léon theatrically kneels, five or six sisters join her.

Mother Saint-Raphaël stands and the hush of her sandals is the only sound as she walks over to the postulant and stares. "Look at me," the prioress says.

Mariette is still. She seldom breathes. Even in her eyes there is no travel.

Mother Saint-Raphaël picks up Mariette's unused fork and hears the sisters gasp as she tests a tine against Mariette's cheek.

She doesn't flinch.

Experimentally, the prioress scrawls the fork down Mariette's neck and hears the silence behind her as she presses harder on the habit until she is holding the fork threateningly against Mariette's left breast. She thinks about stabbing it to demonstrate her seriousness, but then thinks further and Mother Saint-Raphaël takes the fork away and silently prays for God's forgiveness as she turns to say the blessing after meals.

All the sisters then rise up and pray while Mariette stays as she was. All observe the blood dripping from her palms.

Mother Saint-Raphaël slowly walks to the hallway, but only a half-dozen sisters follow. She turns with great irritation and shouts, "*Christ* commands you to leave!"

Hands touch down in the blood covenant as the sisters pass out of the dining hall.

All through the night the Great Silence is torn.

Second rising.

*   *   *

Easy water rustles over stones beneath a Queen Anne's lace of ice.

Warmer, and a southerly breeze. Cathedrals of clouds just above the horizon.

Hurrying sandals in the hallway.

Choiring and starshine and trickling snow.

Mass of Saints Perpetua and Felicitas, Martyrs.

Sister Sabine is on her haunches by a Guernsey cow, drilling hot milk into a tin pail. She props her head on the hide and prays to the blurred stain of blood on the back of her hand.

Sheep whose wool is tan as slush herd against the flitched boards of a fodder shed until Sister Saint-Luc walks out with a great load of cornstalks, a blood cross on her forehead. All follow her to the hurdle.

Dr. Claude Baptiste is in his Kashmir overcoat as he smokes his fifth cigarette of the morning and walks in the priest's yard just behind the high walls of the priory. Everywhere the snow seems blue. Eastward there is rain. Tilting his back into a poplar trunk, he follows a gray braid of smoke as it softly breaks against a tree limb and disappears. *Youth*, he thinks. *Trust. Faith. Ambition.* He hears kitchen noise, and then he hears the old priest falter out of his house and ask, "Shall we go then?"

Sister Aimée is hustling down the hallway toward the oratory and hesitating here and there to wait for Mariette, who walks without hurry and with great hurt, one white-bandaged hand touching its way along the high white wall, one hand tendering her left side.

Thirty sisters are lining up for Terce at the oratory doors and are trying not to dishonor the postulant with sudden prying, but Sister Honoré clenches her thick waist in her arms and frankly stares until Mariette hobbles by, and then the choirmistress unblanks her eyes and bluntly taps the castanets twice and the great doors open.

Sister Aimée has not prepared Mariette for the men in the prioress's suite. Père Marriott is sitting broodingly at the grand pecan desk in a fresh cassock, and he is as absent as an overcoat hung on a chair as he silently turns pages of Sister Marguerite's handwriting. And her father is there, too, in a pitch-black suit and vest and ankle-high shoes, putting Sister Aimée's infirmary report in the bookcase, his wreath of dark hair trained with a floral pomade, a half-inch of cigarette seemingly forgotten between his fingers.

Elaborate rains lash at the windowpanes and dulled sunshine sketches reeds on the floor. Mother Saint-Raphaël heavily positions herself against the chintz pillows of the sofa and holds Mariette in a hostile glare as Sister Aimée walks in with a hand towel and china bowl and pitcher, and puts them on a sill.

Warily skirting his eyes from Mariette, Dr. Baptiste sucks hard on the cigarette and kills it in a half-filled water glass while saying, "She'll have to take off her clothes."

Everything goes unsaid for a while. Mariette hides her hands in her sleeves and hoards her modesty until she asks, "Are you trying to turn it into a disease?"

Mother Saint-Raphaël says, "We have no competence in these matters. We have been like a household with a hundred opinions about an illness but no certainty. We need the verdict of a doctor. We need to be convinced that there is no natural explanation for these wonderful phenomena. When there is no other alternative, then perhaps we shall call them miraculous."

"We are only here to see," Père Marriott assures Mariette. "We shall try to be indifferent and serene, untroubled by whatever facts we turn up and friendly to whatever deductions those facts provide."

Mariette steps out of one roped sandal and the other and then takes off the stockings that hide her foot bandagings. Père Marriott gets up with difficulty and stands at a flecked and fractured window in order to give her privacy, but Dr. Baptiste washes his hands in the china bowl and skeptically peers at Mariette as she peels the headscarf away from her tangling brown hair. She gazes out at the wings of rain in flight across the horse paddock as she unties the cincture and gets out of her habit, and turns to her father in her nakedness. "*Je vous en prie,*" she says. At your service.

Her father turns the trick card of his smile as he stares at her and dries his palms, then tosses the hand towel aside and walks up to Mariette. She blushes in humiliation as she feels his hand and his right thumb bluntly stroking the rib just beneath her left breast. She hears him say to Sister Aimée and Mother Saint-Raphaël, "You'll see there is no 'hand-width laceration.' Even no scarring."

Each of them is hushed for a moment and Dr. Baptiste takes Mariette's left wrist in his hand and stares into her flashing eyes. Without looking away, he says, "Have you scissors, Sister Aimée?"

She gives him a pair and he begins roughly cutting through the hand bandages.

Underneath is blood as thick as a red wax seal. Touching its hardness with great curiosity, her father asks, "Does that hurt?"

She flinches but doesn't say.

Dr. Baptiste turns to the priest, but he seems to be in prayer, so he hesitantly says to Mother Saint-Raphaël, "And now what I'll have to do is tear just a bit of this away. Like a child picks a scab."

"Yes," she says. "You may proceed."

"Try water," Mariette says.

"Excuse me?" he says.

She walks away from him and past Sister Aimée to the china bowl where he'd washed his hands, and she presses hers underwater and holds them there. Tears blur her eyes at the hot sting of pain as the blood feebly unplaits and swims, and then she lifts up her hands again.

Dr. Baptiste goes over and interestedly picks up a hand towel and hastily scrubs her left palm. And he is pleased as he commands the old priest to look.

Père Marriott hunches over her hands in the half light. He urgently finds his brass-rimmed eyeglasses and holds them up and peers at her hands again. The blood and the holes have disappeared.

She tells him, "Christ took back the wounds."

She expects her father to stare at her with fear and astonishment, but he is, as always, frank and unimpressed, as firm and practical as a clock. "And your feet?" he asks.

"I have no wounds."

"Even that is miraculous!" Père Marriott says.

Dr. Baptiste smirks at him and then at Mother Saint-Raphaël. "You all have been duped."

The priest insists, "Explain it to them!"

Mariette flatly says, "What God freely gave me has just as freely been taken away."

"Christ talks to her," her father says. "The Devil strikes her when she tries to pray. She is always saying preposterous things; that's why we don't get along."

She turns to Mother Saint-Raphaël and says, "Whatever I told you was true," but the prioress frowns at her in the fullness of sorrow and says, "You disappoint me, Mariette."

Sister Aimée folds the hand towels and hurriedly takes away the china bowl.

"Shall I go now?" Dr. Baptiste asks.

Mother Saint-Raphaël's face is hidden behind her hand when she answers. "Yes, Doctor. Thank you. We have investigated this quite enough." And then she says, "You stay, Mariette."

When she and the postulant are alone, Mother Saint-Raphaël shifts a chintz pillow and pats a sofa cushion beside her. She stares impassively at Mariette as she sits. She says, "That was simply political, what I said—that you disappoint me. I personally believe that what you say happened did indeed happen. We could never prove it, of course. Skeptics will always prevail. God gives us just enough to seek Him, and never enough to fully find him. To do more would inhibit our freedom, and our freedom is very dear to God."

Mariette is trying not to cry, but she can feel her mouth tremble as she asks, "Are you sending me away?"

"Yes. We are."

"I have always dreamed . . ."

She is stilled when the prioress touches her knee. Mother Saint-Raphaël tells her, "God sometimes wants our desire for a religious vocation but not the deed itself." She then gets up with difficulty and gives half her weight to her cane. "I'll go get Sister Agnès."

Endless rains make a garden of the window glass, reeds and herbs and periwinkles. Mariette sketches them with a nail as she dismally looks outside, and then she hears the door open and sees Sister Agnès in the hallway. "I'll just be getting your things," she says.

Mariette says nothing. She simply waits like an intricate memory as Sister Agnès heavily backs into the room hauling a ship's trunk along the floor. And then Mariette again gets into Mrs. Baptiste's wedding gown of white Holland cloth and watered silk.

"You're still lovely," Sister Agnès says.

"Thank you."

Sister Agnès grins at her. "I'm the first to get you girls when you join us, and I'm the one you go to when you're getting out. Hatched by me; dispatched by me. I'm an important person here."

"You are."

"We were talking about it, Sister Zélie and me. You put one over on us."

Mariette angles her head and snags an ivory comb through her hair. She twinges and holds her hand.

"Are you hurt, dear?"

"Christ let me keep the pain."

Sister Agnès gazes at her. She thinks without a path. She finally says, "Your father's in the priest's house. Waiting."

"Well, goodbye," Mariette says.

"We aren't but just a few of us fit to stay here."

"Well, you've all been very kind," she says.

"You think so? Even now?"

"Oh yes," she says. "You let God use you."

She goes into the oratory and genuflects toward Christ in the tabernacle before unlatching the door in the oaken grille and walking out to the high altar, where she genuflects again. She sees Sister Catherine ironing a Lenten chasuble in the sacristy, but she doesn't speak. She passes through the Communion railing and in solemn procession walks out of the church of Our Lady of Sorrows, just as she entered it in August.

*   *   *

And then she is bleakly tottering through the churned slush and mud of the village, her hair in torrents, wintry rain like tines on her face, the white Holland cloth soaked through and hedged with stains. She falls to her hands and knees and just stays there until she sees a frightened girl in a seal coat on a house porch with the noon mail in her hands. The girl makes the sign of the cross as she kneels, and Mariette forlornly gets to her feet and goes forward to her father's house.

Mass of Saint Thomas Aquinas, Confessor.

Mariette puts a houseplant on the sill of a dining room window as children hurry by after school. She sees the children hesitate and stare. She smiles gently but withdraws.

Mass of Saint Francesca of Rome, Widow.

She goes into the rooms upstairs, getting used to them again. She stands in the book and paper chaos of her father's dark-paneled den. Whiskey is in a square crystal decanter. A tumbler is turned upside down on a handkerchief. She chooses a green chintz chair to sit on, resting her wrists atop antimacassars, her heeled shoes paired as if in a store. She prays until God is there.

Mass of Saint Lucy, Virgin, Martyr. 1912.

She's in a housedress and washing dishes at the kitchen sink as a high school boy she's tutoring sits on a stool at a pantry table and tries sentences in his notebook.

She peers outside. The skies are dark. White flakes are fluttering through the trees like torn paper. And yet it is still warm enough that she can hear water trickle under its gray crepe of ice.

She asks him, "Are you ready?"

"I think so."

She sponges a milk glass. "Whom are you looking for?"

The boy hunches over his handwriting and reads, "*Qui est-ce que vous cherchez?*"

"Excellent. And now: What are you waiting for?"

He hunts his answer. "*Qu'est-ce que vous attendez?*"

"*Très bien,*" Mariette says. And then she holds her hands against her apron as if she's suddenly in pain. She cringes and hangs there for a long time, and then the hurt subsides.

She hears him get up from his stool. "Are you okay?" he asks.

She blushes when she turns to him. She tells him, "Yes. Of course."

Mass of Saint Martha, Virgin. 1917.

Dr. Baptiste tilts heavily in his wheelchair in the shaded green yard, his dinner napkin still tucked in his high starched collar, as Mariette walks from the heat of the house with a Japanese tea service on a tray. She puts it on his side table and he pours for himself as she sits in a striped canvas chair. "Would you like some?" he asks.

She smiles and shakes her head no. She takes off her shoes.

"We'll be having tomatoes soon," he says.

Wrens are flying in and out of the trees. She shades her eyes as she looks at the great orange sun going down. She looks at its haul of shadows.

"We'll have tomato Provençale," he says. "And Creole style. With curry." Dr. Baptiste hears only silence from her.

And then he hears Mariette as she softly whispers the *Nunc Dimittis* of Compline.

Mass of Saint Thérèse of Lisieux. 1929.

She stands before an upright floor mirror at forty and skeins hair that is half gray. She pouts her mouth. She esteems her full breasts as she has seen men esteem them. She haunts her milk-white skin with her hands.

Even this I have given you.

Mass of the Conversion of Saint Paul, Apostle. 1933.

She kneels just inside the church of Our Lady of Sorrows, behind the pews of holy old women half sitting with their rosaries, their heads hooded in black scarves. High Mass has ended. Externs are putting out the candles and vacuuming the carpets. And then there is silence, and she opens to Saint Paul: "We are afflicted in every way possible, but we are not crushed; full of doubts, we never despair. We are persecuted but never abandoned; we are struck down but never destroyed. Continually we carry about in our bodies the dying of Jesus, so that in our bodies the life of Jesus may also be revealed."

Easter Vigil, 1937

Dearest Mother Philomène,

> *You are so kind to remember me in your letter and your prayers! And what marvelous news that you've been chosen the new prioress. God surely had a hand in it, as he has in all the decisions there in that holiest of places.*
>
> *Yes, it has indeed been thirty years. Are we such crones as that? I so often think of you and Sister Hermance and the others. Whenever I can get to Vespers, I try to hear your*

voices, and I sigh theatrically and think how glorious it would be to be with you there again.

I still pray the hours and honor the vows and go to a sunrise Mass. (Each day I thank God for the Chrysler automobile, though I hate the noise.) I tidy the house and tend the garden and have dinner with the radio on. Even now I look out at a cat huddled down in the adder's fern, at a fresh wind nagging the sheets on the line, at hills like a green sea in the east and just beyond them the priory, and the magnificent puzzle is, for a moment, solved, and God is there before me in the being of all that is not him.

And yet sometimes I am so sad. Even when I have friends over often for tea or canasta, there is a Great Silence here for weeks and weeks, and the Devil tells me the years since age seventeen have been a great abeyance and I have been like a troubled bride pining each night for a husband who is lost without a trace.

Children stare in the grocery as if they know ghostly stories about me, and I hear the hushed talk when I hobble by or lose the hold in my hands, but Christ reminds me, as he did in my greatest distress, that he loves me more, now that I am despised, than when I was so richly admired in the past.

And Christ still sends me roses. We try to be formed and held and kept by him, but instead he offers us freedom. And now when I try to know his will, his kindness floods me, his great love overwhelms me, and I hear him whisper, Surprise me.